ZAN

ZAN

— stories —

SUZI EHTESHAM-ZADEH

DZANC
BOOKS

DZANC BOOKS

2580 Craig Rd.
Ann Arbor, MI 48103
www.dzancbooks.org

Library of Congress Cataloging-in-Publication Data TK

ISBN: 9781950539932
First US edition: June 2024
Interior design by Michelle Dotter
Cover design by Steven Seighman

Grateful acknowledgment is made to the editors of the publications in which the following stories first appeared (some in slightly different form):

"Stealthy Freedom" published by *The Georgia Review*, special Southern Post-Colonial issue, April 15, 2022.
"Venus Furtiva" published by Gertrude Press Issue #26, May 17, 2018.
"The Baboon" published by *Fiction International 50: Fool: Fool* (Volume 50), October 16, 2017. (Honorable mention in *The Best American Short Stories* 2018)
"Ghabeleh Hamleh" published by *Hektoen International: A Journal of Medical Humanities*, Volume 9, Issue 4, October 2017.
"Azadi" published by *Five: 2: One Magazine*, 16th print edition, May 25, 2017.
"Coming Out, Going Under" published by *Narrative Northeast*, June 2014.
"Dying in America" published by *Foundling Review*, May 2011.

Printed in the United States of America

10 9 8 7 6 5 4 3 2 1

CONTENTS

For the courageous women of Iran

She can be like a wind-up doll
with two glass eyes and a body stuffed with straw
and glimpse her own world from within a cloth-lined box

She can lie there for years, asleep
surrounded by lace and sequins
and with each slight touch of a lascivious hand
she can cry out, for no reason at all
Oh, how lucky I am!

~ Forough Farrokhzad

PREFACE

IN MY ROLE AS A TEACHER OF LITERATURE, I have often been confronted with questions about the value of fiction. My answer always includes a variation on the famous line about fiction being less strange than reality. This is something I wholeheartedly believe, and it is the reason I write. Like all writers, I grapple with reality when I put words on a page, and part of what drives me is the desire to render it in a form that is more palpable and easier to absorb, not only for my reader, but for myself. This, in simple terms, has been the impetus behind the stories in *Zan*.

No single book, whether fiction or nonfiction, can ever claim to fully capture a whole reality, much less one as complex and important as the Zan, Zendegi, Azadi (Woman, Life, Freedom) movement that is ongoing in Iran. When I began writing these stories, the movement was nothing more than an underground tremor. Midway through my work on the manuscript, the tremor broke through the surface when a young Kurdish woman was arrested for a hijab violation and died while in custody. At this writing, at least 600 Iranian women and men have died in the Iranian government's brutal crackdown on protesters, and an estimated 22,000 have been detained and could face death sentences. Narges Mohammadi, the recipient of the 2023 Nobel Peace Prize for her activism on behalf of Iranian women, has begun a hunger strike in Evin Prison. A potential global conflict has erupted in the Middle East, and Iran is deeply embroiled in it. All of this seems to leave my collection lying in the dust.

A work of fiction should not have to come with disclaimers, but I feel the need to offer one. Although I spent the first two decades of my life in Iran and remain deeply connected to my homeland, I reside in the United States. I cannot claim that my work accurately portrays the political situation in Iran, nor can I speak for the Zan, Zendegi, Azadi movement, nor do I represent the women who are participating in that movement. My goal is less lofty, and I hope more honest: to provide a lens through which my readers might view a complex reality and bring it up close. A second, and perhaps more important, goal is to pay tribute to Iranian women—*zan*—who have been a source of inspiration to me throughout my life.

ZAN

LAST NIGHT BEFORE CLIMBING INTO BED, you found yourself studying your reflection in the mirror. Your face, you noticed, is shaped like a melting heart. The eyelids have grown hooded, the once-rounded cheeks have sagged, the contours are now difficult to find. You weren't bothered by these visible signs of aging. Your identity has never been tied up in your physical appearance, and the older you get, the less important it seems. It wasn't signs of aging you were looking for when you studied your reflection. You were looking for a roadmap of your years on this earth.

In your dream last night, a small figure was walking across a desert landscape, looking up at a vast star-laden sky. You saw the scene from above, like a high-angle shot in a film, but even from so far away you could tell that the figure was a woman. Suddenly, in that way dreams have of blurring lines, the desert morphed into your face and the tiny figure became you, walking across the landscape of your own skin. When you woke up this morning, it occurred to you that your face shares a topography with your country: a dry and rugged surface dotted with dark patches where the sun has punished it, furrows and ruts snaking up from all sides, brittle, windswept hair that looks like an orchard after desertification, eyes that have lost their luster like the bodies of water in your homeland that are becoming toxic and shrinking. Iran is etched into your skin.

Although you have traveled abroad on several occasions, you have never lived anywhere else, nor have you ever wanted to. For all its faults, Iran is where your heart is, and where you will remain until you die. You do not say this out of patriotic fervor. It's hard to feel patriotic when you have lived more than two-thirds of your life under a government you can't support—one that fractured your family and scattered it across the planet, one that ripped your identity apart, one that does not recognize your worth, one that forces you to hide not only your body, but your soul, your womanhood, your very essence.

You feel a great deal of anger toward Iran's leaders, and you carry this anger around with you. But you cannot feel anger at Iran itself, nor at its people. You understand that people are often, if not always, victims of their leaders. Even the most casual look at your country's history proves that this has been the case with Iran. The injustices you and your people have faced have been the fault of heartless and corrupt individuals, most of them men.

These men have not always been kind to women. And yet, your identity as a woman is inextricable from your identity as an Iranian. You are *zan*: an Iranian woman—and that is its own particular thing. The Iranian woman has been viewed through many lenses over the course of her history: she has been maligned and ridiculed, scorned and pitied, glamorized, exoticized, and revered. You do not pay much attention to these labels, and you are neither proud nor ashamed to identify as an Iranian woman. Right now, identifying as a zan has become more crucial than ever. It has become essential to your sanity and your survival.

You sometimes think of Iran itself as a woman. She is a big-hearted, maternal woman with a boundless ability to love; a competent, resourceful woman who can produce a delicious meal when there is nothing left in the pantry; an ancient woman who possesses the kind of wisdom that can only come with age. Her origins go back thousands of years, and she spans many eras. Your life is not even a dewdrop in her vast ocean.

Throughout your life, Iran has behaved toward you the way a mother does. She has cradled you, protected you, challenged you, embarrassed you, scolded you, and punished you, often cruelly and unjustly. When you were a child, she sent you out into streets and orchards during the day to play freely under the sun, and at night she told you fairy tales about kings and queens and empires. When you were a teenager, she dressed you in bikinis and sent you to the beach, drove you to boutiques where you could buy miniskirts, painted your face with makeup, pointed you toward bars and discotheques, and taught you how to perform a certain kind of womanhood she believed in at the time.

Just as you were approaching adulthood, she yanked all of that away from you overnight. She replaced the tales about kings and queens with tales about ogres and monsters. She filled you with guilt for your past actions and presented you with a different concept of womanhood. She made you feel ashamed of your blossoming female body and commanded you to hide it from view. She drove you indoors and put you under constant surveillance. She gave you a different set of rules to follow, enforcing them with the fear of incarceration and bodily harm.

Later in your life, she became cantankerous, rigid, and controlling. She began to fight with her former friends and replaced them with new friends. People you once trusted were branded as evil; people you had always been wary of were welcomed into your home. She created hostility and tension throughout the neighborhood, filling you with shame and fear.

She has not always been a good mother, and at times you have wanted to abandon her. But then you remember the powerful poetry she once wrote, the enchanting songs she once sang, the graceful way she once danced, the beautiful, intricate objects she once made with her own hands. She is your mother, and when she is sick, you feel a duty to nurse her back to health.

She is very sick right now. She is determined to put forth a show of strength, but you can see through her bluster, and you know she is secretly fighting for her life. The virus that swept across the planet tore through her like a marauding army, and she did not prove to be a match for it. She is used to invaders: she has been subjected to them throughout her history. From the Greeks and Macedonians to the Mongols and Arabs, from the British and Soviets to the Americans and Iraqis, everyone has wanted a piece of her. But the virus was a different kind of invader, and it took a toll on her.

And there are countless other plagues being visited upon her right now. The air she breathes is filthy, she is engulfed by scorching heat, there is not enough water, and food is scarce. Oil and chemicals have leaked into her soil, making it infertile. She lacks the resources and the strength to feed her children, and they, too, are growing ill. And yet she refuses medicine, insisting that she does not need anyone's help. She faces very real threats from outsiders who scorn and mistrust her, but she continues to provoke their ire. Inside her own borders there is unrest everywhere, but she chooses to look away.

In the face of these challenges and others, she can't seem to decide who she wants to be or how she wants to behave. The eyes of the world are on her, and she is fearful. But instead of conquering her fears—or even admitting to them—she buries them or masks them with false bravado. In her insecurity, she lashes out at those who are the most vulnerable and those who love her most. She seems to have lost her way.

You are aware that you cannot heal her alone—that you must turn to others for help. Being of advanced age, perhaps you should feel that your power is diminishing. But somehow, the opposite is happening. You are not focusing on your past suffering, and you are not thinking about what you have lost. Instead, you are remembering what it was like to be young and free, what it was like to laugh and love and believe in the beauty of the world. People your age are often bogged down by memories, but you are turning your mind around, away from the past and toward the future. As murky as it might seem, it doesn't scare you.

Tomorrow, you will study your face in the mirror again, and you will love the landscape you see, despite the many signs of trauma and age written upon it. But you will not focus on your reflection for too long before you turn away from it and take yourself out into the streets. There, you will join your many sisters who are fighting with all their might to restore your mother to health. You are all being targeted, but you will show up with targets on your backs. You have come too far and suffered too much to turn back now.

STEALTHY FREEDOM *

E ACH DAY BEFORE SHE leaves her home, Saghi drapes herself
in flowing sheets of cotton and muslin and silk. She does so
with an artist's eye, knowing how the folds will fall along her
shoulders, where to tie the knot so it will reveal a suggestive triangle
of flesh at the base of her neck, how the fabric will form an arrow
down her back that will point straight to her hips and sway with
them as she walks. She knows what colors and patterns best com-
plement her complexion, and she knows how to arrange the fabric
around her face so that her best features—high cheekbones, full lips,
arched eyebrows—will spring arrestingly to life. Always there is some
hair showing, and this, too, is strategic. A few wispy strands must
be loosened from beneath the top line of the headscarf, just enough
to suggest the luscious tresses that lie beneath. The daily process of
draping herself in fabric has given her an intimate relationship with
her body.

---

* In 2014, an Iranian woman posted a picture of herself on Facebook that was taken
while she was walking down the streets of London without a hijab. Shortly afterwards,
an online movement titled "My Stealthy Freedom" was born. As part of this movement,
women took photos and videos of themselves appearing in public in Iran without the
mandatory hijab and posted them on Facebook. The movement spread rapidly, soon
reaching over 1 million followers. This story is loosely based on that movement. It is set
shortly before the death of Mahsa Amini in 2022, which sparked the Women, Life, Freedom movement that is ongoing today.

Today she takes special pleasure in her preparations. After she emerges from the shower, she pats herself dry and rubs a generous coating of rosewater over her skin. Then she stands before the mirror and admires herself, marveling at her slim waistline, the bulge of her hips, the delicate curve of her breasts. She watches herself in the mirror as she snaps on her bra, slips on her panties, and slides nylon stockings over her slender legs. She selects a silky, tight-fitting blouse from her closet and watches herself do up each snap, beginning with the bottom one and making her way up to the snap that rests right below her cleavage. She will remain in her blouse and stockings until just before leaving, when she will perform the final stage: the act of draping herself.

Wearing makeup in public is usually not wise, as the morality police have become more ubiquitous lately, lurking on street corners and pulling women aside to arrest them, or at the very least shame them, for hijab violations. But makeup is essential today, and she delights in her own shrewdness as she applies it. She doesn't need foundation for her flawless skin, but she paints her eyelids like a canvas, applying a soft arc of copper-colored eyeshadow, a thin line of kohl, a gentle brushing with mascara to accentuate her lashes. She will keep her sunglasses on until the critical moment arrives. The bright red lipstick, which the morality police refer to as "martyr's blood," cannot be applied until later. It will go into her purse until it is time to put it on.

Next she turns her attention to her hair, a thick mane of ebony that falls just below her shoulders. She cannot wear it loose because this will lessen the effect of what she is about to do, and the fashionable high ponytail she usually wears beneath her hijab also won't be practical. She opts for a large butterfly clip. Holding it in one hand, she gathers up her hair in the other and snaps the clip into place.

Saghi has been wearing a headscarf since the age of nine, so putting one on before she leaves home is as natural to her as putting on shoes. Removing it is equally natural for her; she does so with one swift movement as soon as she crosses the threshold and is safely away from the eyes of the authorities. Today, though, the removal of her headscarf will be a willful act of defiance, so it must carry weight. She must remove it in a manner that is ceremonious, unrepentant, combative. She is aware that the action will come with great risk. Other women have been caught while performing the action and accused of what the government calls "the crime of corruption and prostitution." Some have suffered grave consequences: arrest and interrogation, lashes, decades-long sentences in Evin Prison. Her pulse quickens as she considers these consequences, but she is resolved. She sits down on the bed to await the phone call.

☙

Paradoxically, the ritual of draping herself always makes Saghi feel proud to be a woman. She knows many kinds of women in the Islamic Republic, and they fill her with admiration. There are women who wield tremendous power and whose husbands cower before them. Women who appear docile, but who defy their given roles in subtle but vital ways. Women who have tasted just enough freedom to whet their appetites for more. Women whose lives were thrown off course by a government they did not choose, who adapted and learned to curl their existence around injustice, who kept growing and thriving even when the cards were stacked against them. Women who uphold tradition and women who fly in its face. Women who languish in prison for speaking their minds and women who stand outside the prison gates and raise their fists for justice. All these women must drape themselves in fabric, and each does so with her own subtle motives in mind.

She is aware that women in the Western world are speaking out against the men who abuse them, and she is happy for these women. They are her sisters. But they did not grow up, as she did, in the birthplace of miniature painting, so they fail to recognize that the true picture is often hidden in the fine details. They paint the women who drape themselves the way a child might paint them, with simple, clumsy brushstrokes, giving them all the same face of resignation and the same shapeless garment that hides their shoulders, hips, and breasts—even their hands and feet. They don't understand that the abuse these women face does not begin and end with their hijab. It is deeper, more tangled, and more insidious. Simple words like "me too" are not strong enough weapons for Saghi and her draped sisters.

Her parents made a provocative choice when they named her Saghi, and the audacity of her name has always gratified her. It is a name that raises eyebrows because it hearkens back to an earlier time, a time that is now seen as sinful and toxic. The name was taken from the saghi who appear frequently in the ghazals of Hafez, the great Sufi poet and mystic. On the surface the word denotes female wine-servers, but Hafez's saghi were far more than mere women. They were vehicles of truth—women whose seductive femininity put men in a trance that led them to god. The god in the ghazals of Hafez is not the Allah of the filthy bearded men who run the country, but a higher, airier kind of god. The older she gets, the more Saghi strives to be worthy of her lusty, life-affirming name.

She is thankful to have been raised by parents who bequeathed their pre-revolutionary culture to her—parents who still read poetry, drink alcohol, and believe in dancing and music and sex. Thanks to them, and to the Internet, she grew up listening to female singing voices, forbidden now unless they are performing for female audiences or blended with male voices in a chorus. Saghi has been told that she possesses a heavenly voice, and she sings often: in the shower, at family gatherings, at the parties she sometimes attends. If she could sing when she walked down the street draped in fabric, she would mesmerize men like a siren.

Today it is not her singing voice she will use to assert her power. Instead, she will use the strongest weapon she possesses, which also happens to be the very symbol of her oppression.

Ↄↄ

The phone call comes promptly at ten a.m., as planned. Saghi does not really know Neguin, the woman on the other end of the line. She has only met her once, briefly, on a street in front of Azad University where they are both students. The meeting between them was arranged by a mutual friend, and as soon as Saghi laid eyes on Neguin, she felt a spark of kinship. Roughly her own height and build and draped in similar fabric, Neguin might have been mistaken for her twin if the two of them were seen from a distance. But when she heard Neguin voice her opinions without fear and watched her toss her head back in genuine laughter, Saghi knew that this woman had ascended to a higher plane of self-realization. It fills her with glee to imagine her male professors struggling to keep their composure when confronted with classrooms full of women like Neguin.

Now Neguin is on the other end of her cell phone, and Saghi's heart thumps as she pushes the button to answer the call. After a brief exchange of greetings, Neguin goes straight to the matter at hand. "Are you going to be ready today?" she asks.

"Yes, of course," Saghi replies. "But you haven't told me where I am going."

"Do you know Laleh Park?"

"Yes, I do. What time should I be there?"

"We are aiming for the early afternoon. It is safest right after the shops and offices close for the afternoon. There will still be people in the park and on the streets, but the guards and patrols will be on their break. Can you make it at 14:30?"

"Absolutely. I will be there."

"Good! Don't fail us."

Saghi cannot be sure she won't fail in the mission, but she sputters, "I won't!" and ends the call.

The time has come for the final stage of the draping process; the stage that immediately precedes her exit from the house. She keeps an assortment of *roopoosh*, Islamic outerwear, beside the front door: a summer roopoosh made of flouncy cotton, a form-fitting roopoosh in daring colors, a boutique roopoosh with a fashionable cut that falls just above the knee. Today she chooses the most comfortable and least conspicuous roopoosh she has, a simple beige one with tortoise-shell buttons down the front. She knows right away which headscarf she will wear with it: the large gauzy one with a leopard-skin print. Watching herself in the full-length mirror in the hallway, she billows the scarf out over her head, wraps it around her neck once, then tosses the loose right end over her left shoulder. She picks up the small purse in which she has placed her cell phone, her wallet, and the tube of red lipstick, and settles it across her torso. One last head-to-toe inspection in the hallway mirror, and she steps outside.

જી

When Saghi leaves her home on an ordinary day, whether for work or school or shopping, she goes out with her chin held high and her shoulders straight. She has heard that in the days before the revolution, when her mother was her age, women were subjected to brazen wolf whistles and catcalls when they walked down the street. In the Islamic Republic it is considered vulgar for men to reveal their baser urges, so they have learned to restrain the animals that live inside them. It amuses Saghi when she feels their furtive eyes straining to follow her movements, to take in as much of her as possible in their peripheral vision. Their suppressed reactions, the combination of fear and awe that her approach inspires, sometimes gives her a rush of power. But the stakes are high today, and she can't be certain what kinds of feelings she will provoke.

The air in Tehran is usually thick and fetid, but today a clear blue expanse stretches above her as she makes her way toward the bus stop. The bus is crowded, but bus riders in the city are used to minding their own business, and no one pays attention to her when she boards. With her dull roopoosh and her makeup hidden behind sunglasses, she is just another woman on a bus—an office worker, a daughter, a young wife.

She sits down in an aisle seat, leaving the window seat beside her empty. It is the only empty seat left on the bus, and when a man gets on a few stops later, she gets up to allow him to slide into the window seat so she won't have to climb over him to get out. The man does not seem interested in her at first, but after a few minutes he turns to her and speaks.

"I take this bus every day at this hour," he says, "but I have never seen you before. Where are you going, sister? You can't be shopping, since all the stores are closed until this evening."

It irks Saghi when men she doesn't know call her "sister," but she doesn't allow her voice to betray her annoyance. "My aunt lives near Laleh Park. How many stops are left before that one?" As soon as the question leaves her mouth, she realizes her mistake. "She just moved here from Isfahan," she adds. "It's my first time visiting her."

"Three more stops," the man says. Saghi thinks she sees playful suspicion on his face, but when he turns away from her and looks out the window, she knows she is safe. He nudges her arm and says "Next one" when her stop is approaching, and they exchange a friendly smile as she gets up to exit.

Laleh Park is located in a bustling downtown district, an incongruous spot of green in the otherwise grimy city center. Saghi remembers coming here on a few occasions as a child, and although she has not been back in years, she has a sudden visual memory of the park's layout. She heads toward the middle of the park where she knows there is a large fountain, expecting to find people congregated there. But the area is not the way she remembers it. On either side of the fountain there are people hurrying home for the afternoon rest period: older women struggling with heavy shopping bags, mothers pulling children by the hand to get them to walk faster, men with their heads down, puffing on cigarettes. A few bloated city pigeons, their feathers the color of soot, look up at her indifferently for a moment, then continue pecking at debris in the grass.

She must find a better spot. She remembers that the park has a large playground, and she turns in that direction. A group of children are crouched down in the dirt beneath the slide, playing a game with stones, and as she draws closer, she notices that a few of them are girls. They are wearing headscarves, so she takes their ages to be above nine, the age at which the hijab becomes mandatory. The children do not seem to notice her presence, or if they do, they think nothing of it.

Over to one side of the playground there is a cluster of park benches. She surveys the people sitting on them: mothers and fathers watching their children, youths on their cell phones, elderly couples out for a stroll, workers pausing to rest before they continue their path toward home. Beyond the benches there is a stone walkway lined with cedar trees, and two young mothers are pushing their children in strollers along it. On the far side of the path, she can spot the street that runs along this end of the park. Pedestrians walk with purpose along the sidewalks, and cars and motorcycles zigzag down the center of the street, their nasal horns drowning out the laughter of the children on the playground.

She is debating whether to sit down on a park bench when her cell phone rings, and the screen tells her it is Neguin. She skips the greeting this time, and just asks, "How does it look?"

Saghi isn't sure she understands the question, so she responds with a question of her own: "How is it supposed to look?"

"Count how many people you can see."

Saghi looks around her and does a quick inventory of the playground area, the park benches, the people on the stone walkway, and the pedestrians on the adjacent street. "About twenty or twenty-five," she says.

"Men or women?"

"Both. And a few children."

"Children are no problem! Children are great! But I hope there are at least that many people when the right moment comes. Fewer than twenty would be a shame."

At the mention of "the right moment," Saghi's heart begins to quicken. She covers her nervousness by blurting out another question. "Is everyone else ready?"

"Neda is ready, and so is Afsaneh. They are in touch with the others, and they're all standing by. I'm waiting to hear from Soussan. She had to walk because the bus line to her spot wasn't running today. Her spot is Tabiat Bridge, so it is crucial that she be there."

Saghi knows Tabiat Bridge well. It is the largest pedestrian bridge in Tehran, spanning a wide highway and connecting two of the city's most frequented parks. The bridge is full of people all day long, even during the high heat of naptime. She is astonished that anyone would have the courage to select that spot. "Isn't that dangerous?" she asks.

"Yes, of course it is!" Neguin scoffs. "But Tabiat Bridge is an important symbol because it was designed by a woman. Did you know that?"

Saghi can't bring herself to lie. "I didn't, actually," she says. "But I did know that the design was inspired by a tree, which is why it has

that huge post in the middle that looks like a trunk with branches."
As soon as she utters this sentence, she realizes it is trivial and irrelevant. This is not the time for small talk.

Neguin remains silent for a few beats, then says, "Oh! I think
this is Soussan calling now! That means everyone is ready to go. All
you have to do is find the right spot and wait for the signal. Remember, you're all going to do this at around the same time, and I'm going
to gather all the photos and videoclips and post them together, like
a huge flood."

Now Saghi's heart is thumping so hard she can feel it in her
throat and her temples. A boy from the playground looks up at her,
and she wonders for a moment if he can hear her heartbeat. Realizing how foolish this thought is, she gives him a broad smile, and he
smiles back.

What is the right spot? How can she tell? She thinks back on
the videos she has seen of women in Tabriz, Abadan, Isfahan, Shi-
raz, even the holy city of Qom. The video of a stunning beauty, no
more than sixteen years old, who strides into the middle of a subway
car and shouts, "*Look at us, women of the West! Are you impressed?*"
The video of two women who stand together in the center of Azadi
Square, under the famous monument, and scream, "*Azadi means
freedom, and* this *is my freedom!*" The video of an older woman, probably in her sixties, who walks up the front steps of the Parliament
building, turns toward the street, and shouts, "*They got Fereshteh, and
Pari became her voice. They got Pari, and Simin became her voice. They
got Simin, and Mojgan became her voice. They got Mojgan, and I have
become her voice.*"

These women had made careful choices of the general locale they
would go to, but at the last moment they had resorted to instinct
when choosing the exact spot. She mustn't overthink. Instead, she
must calm her beating heart and try her best to be natural.

She crosses through the playground in the direction of the street, and as she does so, she lifts the lipstick from her purse and streaks it across her lips. She drops the tube back into her purse, removes her sunglasses and drops them in there too, then retrieves her cell phone. She isn't practiced at filming herself, but the quality of the video is not important. It is the subject matter—the action itself—that counts.

The signal comes just as she is passing in front of a park bench full of men. Without pausing to think, she reaches up and with a single, deft motion pulls her headscarf down around her shoulders and frees her hair from the butterfly clip. The clip falls to the ground, and she leaves it there. She points her cell phone camera at her made-up face, at her full red lips, at her hair. She can't feel a breeze, so she shakes her head from side to side to show the full effect of her loose hair. Still training the cell phone on herself, she uses her free hand to unbutton her roopoosh, points the camera at her upper body, and films her tight-fitting blouse. Just as she is about to film her hair again, a breeze starts up, as if on cue. She lifts the scarf from her shoulders and holds it aloft until it catches the wind, then lets it go, filming it as it rises toward the treetops. Then she points the camera back at her face, films her smile, and pushes the red button at the bottom of her screen. She quickly dials Neguin on WhatsApp and sends the clip over to her.

A few meters away on the playground, a child gives a frightened cry and begins running toward the park benches. Saghi freezes for a moment, but then she notices that the other children are looking up at her with wonder and expectation on their faces. One of them, a girl of about ten who is wearing a school-issued hijab, begins clapping. Slowly, hesitantly, a few other children join in. She turns the cell phone toward the playground, films the children, and sends the clip to Neguin.

Now, suddenly, the people on either side of the playground are in motion. She was wrong—there are far more than twenty people here. She is surrounded by them, and she has the sudden awareness that they are closing in on her, not to harm her, but to protect her. Some begin clapping, and others point their cell phones in her direction to film her. Before long, the roar of clapping hands is all around her: it is coming from the playground, from the cluster of benches, from the stone walkway, even from the street. It occurs to her that this is the first time in her life she has received applause from perfect strangers. Emboldened now, she shouts, "Post this on Instagram! Post it on Facebook! Send it to everyone you know!"

She spins around toward the people who are now surrounding her and points her phone at the constellation of faces. She is not sure what she is filming, but it doesn't matter because everyone around her seems to be filming. The moment will be eternalized.

From one side of the playground, a man is striding angrily in her direction. She has anticipated this, and she has thought about how she will respond. She will not back away from him, but instead stand stock still, as if she were confronting a wild bear. She will fix her eyes on his and challenge him with her glare. She will give him a derisive smile, perhaps even laugh out loud in his face. If he thinks she is being immoral or trying to seduce him, that will be the work of his imagination—and she will tell him so.

He storms toward her, waving an object in her direction. At first she thinks it might be a weapon, but then she realizes it is just a stick he has picked up from the ground. When he is a few feet away, he thrusts the stick at her and snarls, "*Kessaffat*! Filth!"

Saghi has been given no precise script for this situation, but she doesn't need one. She turns her cell phone around and points it at the man, zooming in on his brutish face. "Why are you looking?" she asks defiantly. "Who gave you permission to look?" She moves the cell phone closer to him, so close that it is almost touching him. "You are the one . . . you've got the problem!" She steps toward him until she is close enough for him to see her makeup, smell her perfume, feel her breath. "You are the one who is *kessaffat*! Men are not supposed to ogle women, didn't you know that? And if you're aroused by my hair, I think you've got a problem!"

The crowd has now gathered around her in a huddle, and they raise their voices to jeer at the man. "*Boro gom sho! Boro pey-karet*! Get lost! Mind your own business!" He begins to back away, shouting as he retreats, "There are laws in this country, you whore!"

"Yes, there are! Believe me, I know that. I am a victim of those laws every day. Let me remind you that there were laws about slavery too. That didn't make it right."

"*Boro! Boro!*" Go! Go! the crowd says in chorus, waving their arms in the man's direction. He puts his hands to his face to shield himself from the cell phones, then drops his head between his shoulders and slinks toward the edge of the park.

Even though she knows he can no longer hear her, Saghi shouts in his direction, her voice rising in pitch. "Go tell Khamenei! Tell him to find me and lock me up. Then you can live with the guilt of what those pigs will do to me."

All around her, cell phones are glinting in the air. Some are filming her, some are filming the retreating man, some are panning around the area and filming the whole scene. Saghi turns her phone back toward her own face. What she says next is not meant for the man; it is for the whole world to hear. She reaches up with her free hand to tousle her hair, then moves it down along the side of her face and across her chest. "This is my hair!" she shrieks, her voice now ecstatic. "This is my face! This is my body! Mine!"

Startled by her own words, she pauses, saves the clip, and forwards it to Neguin. Less than a minute later, her phone begins to ding.

THE BABOON

NIGHT FALLS SUDDENLY IN THE BAGH. It seems to drop down from above without warning, like a curtain closing against the day. Just before the generator is started up and the lights go on, there is a moment when the sky is vast and deep. The stars are so numerous and so immediate that they appear to be in motion, like handfuls of luminescent sand tossed by a celestial giant.

As soon as they spot the artificial light, the moths come immediately, out of nowhere, and hurl themselves toward light bulbs and lanterns. Some of them have wings the size of human hands, and others are tiny and transparent, barely there at all. In their frenzied rush toward the light, some crash into the glass of the light bulbs and lanterns and their wings melt in an instant, leaving their desperate bodies writhing on the scalding surface. Others, mistaking the reflection on the open glasses of alcohol as a light source, are driven into the glowing liquid, where they flutter for a moment, then drown.

Over the years, Pedar-jaan has collected the moths. He has pinned them, with their wings spread open, to pieces of cardboard painted to match the color of the sky and has covered them with glass frames which line the walls of his home in the bagh. He is not a scientist; his interest in the moths has always been purely aesthetic. Roya remembers studying the impaled creatures when she was a child and finding them fearsome even though she knew they were dead and locked inside glass cases. Tonight, as she stands on the balcony of her grandfather's home and witnesses the astonishing transition from the cosmic to the terrestrial—from the vast, star-laden sky to the desperate fluttering of the fragile creatures around the artificial light—she finds the moths beautiful and tragic.

Beyond the balcony, in the distance, Roya can make out the shadowy outlines of the mountains and trees, barely visible behind the curtain of night. These contours have not changed since she was last here as a child, and although she is not surprised by this fact, she feels suddenly moved by it. Almost everything else has changed in the fifteen years she has been away, but this landscape has been the same for generations, perhaps centuries. Pedar-jaan saw this same view as a child, as did his grandfather. Looking at it is like looking back in time.

She pulls her vision in closer and glances across the balcony at her husband Andrew. She wants to tell him about the unchanging tree line, and she wants to see if he is noticing the moths. But Andrew seems lost in his own thoughts, and she decides not to intrude. He doesn't have to see everything through her eyes.

She hears a voice on the balcony behind her and turns to see Farideh, the much younger woman Pedar-jaan married after Roya's grandmother died. Roya had never met Farideh before this morning, but she feels a sudden bond with this woman who takes care of her grandfather, this stranger who now occupies a deeper place within the family than Roya herself. Farideh is wearing an apron and her hair is fastened above the nape of her neck in a tight bun. She stands at the edge of the balcony and bends slightly at the waist in a gesture that is not quite a bow. "*Be-farma-eed sham,*" she says. "Dinner is served."

The gamey smell of lamb hits them full force as they rise from their seats and move from the balcony into the dining room. On the table in front of them sits a veritable feast: mountains of steaming rice with several kinds of khoresh, fresh naan baked in the neighboring village, lamb and chicken kabab; eggplant dolmeh and stuffed grape leaves. They stand at attention and wait until Pedar-jaan is seated before arranging themselves around the table.

Roya cannot quite believe that she is sitting across the table from her grandfather for the first time as an adult. Pedar-jaan has been a gentleman farmer all his life and probably has no more than a sixth-grade education, but she has always considered him the most sophisticated and erudite person she knows. She is so giddy with emotion that she forgets to translate for Andrew—in fact, she almost forgets that her husband is there.

It is Pedar-jaan who finally addresses him. Roya dutifully translates the exchange between her husband and her grandfather.

"Agha-An-de-roo," he says, stumbling over the consonant cluster. "How do you like the Islamic Republic so far?"

Roya translates Pedar-jaan's words exactly, although she finds it curious that he refers to the country this way rather than calling it Iran. Like all the members of her Iranian family, Pedar-jaan is bitterly opposed to the Islamic government that has a stranglehold over the nation. Andrew, too, seems surprised by the question. He looks at Roya quizzically, as if the right answer might be written on her face.

"I haven't seen much in the five days we've been here, but from what I've seen so far, it's a beautiful country."

Pedar-jaan chuckles softly. "I don't see how this dry, forgotten land of ours can seem beautiful to someone from Amreeka. But you must visit the village tomorrow. You do not have villages in your country, I am told."

"I would be honored to go there."

Roya is not certain she knows the correct word for honored, but she manages to transmit her husband's meaning to Pedar-jaan. He looks at Andrew and gives him a smile that carries a touch of disdain.

"It is not an honor, An-de-roo-joon. The villagers are just people, after all. They are not actors in an American movie."

Andrew sits in silence for a minute, trying to interpret the tone behind the old man's words. He swallows audibly. "Of course not," he says. "They don't make American movies about Iranian villagers."

Roya studies her husband across the dinner table. He is trying to look casual, but discomfort glimmers beneath the surface of his expression. His slender body is leaning forward in a way that suggests great interest, but there is tension in his limbs. He has taken great pains with his dress tonight; he looks well-groomed and handsome. His long, sandy-colored hair has been slicked back so he will seem less conspicuously foreign. He is trying.

ⸯ

If anything has disturbed Andrew since their arrival in the Islamic Republic, he has done a good job of hiding it. Roya herself is having more difficulty adjusting. The last time she visited Iran, she was a mere child and didn't have to bother with a hijab—but this time, as the plane was descending toward Imam Khomeini Airport, she was forced to go into the tiny toilet to transform herself before she could enter her country as a woman. In her purse she carried a makeshift roopoosh-roosaree. The headscarf was fashioned from a dull gray fabric remnant she bought at Walmart, and she had found an old raincoat to use as a substitute for a roopoosh, leaving the sash open to avoid accentuating the contours of her body. When she leaned in close to examine her reflection in the plane's distorted bathroom mirror, she barely recognized herself. She looked like a nun wearing a mismatched habit.

She caught Andrew's eye as she navigated the aisle back toward her seat. She could tell that he was startled by the transformation, but true to form, he covered his reaction with an attempt at humor. He flashed her a mock-salacious smile as she sat down beside him. "Wow! You look amazing!" he whispered. "Makes me want to rip all those clothes off and see what's underneath."

"Nice try, Andrew. You know I look ridiculous," she answered.

She was so aware of how ridiculous she looked that she could feel her face burning as they entered the terminal and walked down the long corridor toward border control. Andrew had not undergone a transformation before entering the airport, but somehow, he looked ridiculous too. He was a full head taller than most of the other passengers, and his blond hair, which swirled around his head like a lion's mane, seemed to be a defiant proclamation of his alien presence in the dark-haired crowd.

Even when the border patrol subjected Andrew to an interrogation, he remained as calm as the sphinx.

"Which side will you fight on in the war?"

"Which war?"

"The one that's coming. The United States and Israel against Iran."

"Neither side."

Roya's heart had pounded so violently when she translated this exchange that she felt certain it was visible beneath her roopoosh. Her Farsi was rusty after so many years away, and seeing a Kalashnikov rifle at such close range didn't help to put her at ease. But the customs official had been too fascinated by Andrew to pay much attention to her nervousness or her grammar. His face broke into a toothy smile as he welcomed them both to Iran, sending them directly under the stadium-sized banner that read MARG BAR AMREEKA: *DEATH TO AMERICA.*

On their first foray out into the Tehran streets the next morning, Roya was reminded again how out of touch she was with her country. The women sashayed through the streets in brightly colored scarves draped seductively around their shoulders, exposing lots of hair and drawing attention to their heavily made-up faces. Their roopooshes were form-fitting and ended just above the knee, and beneath the tunics their legs were covered in skin-tight leggings. That same afternoon, Roya went to a surprisingly upscale shopping mall in north Tehran to buy a more contemporary Islamic costume.

Now that she is in her grandfather's bagh, she is finally freed from the absurd costume altogether. Out on her grandfather's balcony tonight, Roya could feel the night breeze fluttering through her hair for the first time since she has been back in Iran, and this, like her memory of the stars and the moths, is helping her to remember that she belongs here, that this is, in a sense, still her home. She spent every summer of her childhood in this bagh in the company of her cousins, riding donkeys, climbing mountains, and picking fruit straight from the trees. Despite decades of tyranny, there is no repressive regime to contend with in this beautiful patch of land nestled in the Zagros Mountains.

⁓

After dinner Farideh invites them back out to the balcony, where she has arranged a low table with a tray that holds a bucket of ice, sliced limes, several clean glasses, and a bottle of araq, moonshine made from fermented raisins. Roya and Andrew sit together on the carpet and lean back against the cushions that line the periphery of the balcony. The mountain air is cold, and they drape themselves with quilts, leaving only their arms exposed so that they can sip their drinks.

Pedar-jaan, who occupies the central spot on the carpet which covers the floor of the balcony, pulls a sweater on. He leans back against the overstuffed cushions that have been arranged along the balcony rail and motions to his wife.

"Farideh-joon," he says, "tell Attah to bring my manqal."

Roya knows that social hierarchies have not changed much in Iran despite the Revolution: the bagh has been in her family since the time of the Qajar dynasty, and was handed down to Pedar-jaan complete with workers from the neighboring village who still labor in the cherry orchards and vineyards under a system that resembles feudalism. Nevertheless, Roya is surprised that her grandfather still has a serving boy and still gives orders to him indirectly through his wife. She has been away for so long that ordering servants no longer seems like a natural human interaction to her.

But she is not surprised by the order itself. Pedar-jaan has been an opium addict since before she was born, and she knows that asking for his manqal after dinner is his custom each night. She witnessed the ritual of opium smoking each summer throughout her childhood, and despite her many years of absence she remembers the routine. The manqal, a bronze opium pit heaped with lumps of red-hot charcoal, will be placed on the carpet in front of Pedar-jaan. After he smokes himself, he will invite the other adults to indulge, motioning for each to approach the manqal in turn.

The perfume of the opium sweeps across the balcony on the night breeze. Roya remembers it distinctly—it is a delicious aroma, pure and organic, like leather or aged wood. Even without smoking she can feel the drug's mesmerizing effect.

After taking a deep hit from his pipe, Pedar-jaan closes his eyes and falls into a brief opium-induced sleep. When he opens his eyes again, he looks directly at Andrew and summons him toward the manqal.

"*Bee-ya, And-e-roo-jaan*," Pedar-jaan says. "Come, Andrew."

Roya has prepared Andrew for this moment, and he knows what to do. He glances at her and smiles, then gets up and seats himself cross-legged on the carpet beside the old man.

Pedar-jaan warms the pipe over the charcoal and lifts it toward Andrew's lips. Roya knows that the gesture is full of meaning—that it signals her grandfather's acceptance of her American husband. Pedar-jaan continues to cradle the pipe while Andrew inhales, keeping the charcoal balanced just above the piece of opium. Andrew holds the smoke inside his lungs for a long time before he lets it out again in a thick and steady stream. He does not cough.

"*Barak'Allah*," Pedar-jaan says, and Roya translates, "Good for you. You learn quickly."

Andrew's eyelids drop closed and he leans back against the cushions. Pedar-jaan lets him rest for a moment, then rouses him gently with a touch on the shoulder and pours him a glass of tea from the teapot sitting on the manqal.

"Roya-jaan, tell him that he must now drink this cup of tea with a lot of sugar, otherwise he might feel nausea." Roya translates, and Andrew accepts the tea.

Next it is Roya's turn to smoke. This is her initiation—the ceremony that marks her passage into adulthood in her grandfather's eyes. She must be graceful. Pedar-jaan places the pipe against her lips and she inhales deeply, bending up all her energy to the feeling of the opium coursing through her body. As soon as it enters her bloodstream her eyelids, too, drop closed against her will. When she opens them again, she cannot calculate how long they have been closed—it could be a few minutes or a full hour. A hush falls over the balcony, or perhaps it is the effect of the opium that makes it seem that way. The moths continue their suicide missions, but now when Roya looks at them, they seem to be traveling in slow motion and their buzzing is barely audible.

Suddenly the silence is broken by the sound of Pedar-jaan clearing his throat, and Roya is jolted to attention. She remembers this sound: her grandfather, a master storyteller, always clears his throat this way before he begins a story. It is obvious that tonight's story is going to be told especially for Andrew, because Pedar-jaan looks directly at him and says, "I want to tell you about a strange thing that happened a few years ago here at the bagh."

Once again Roya forgets for an instant that Andrew cannot understand Farsi. Pedar-jaan pauses and turns toward her. He is waiting for her to translate.

Andrew sits up now with his back against the cushion so that he can pay closer attention. Even though it is Roya's voice he needs to listen to, it is the old man he looks at. And so the story floats across the night sky, circling from Roya's grandfather through Roya herself, and continuing its arc toward her husband.

ɛɔ

"One day, out of the blue, Attah brought a baboon to us," Pedar-jaan begins. "It had been given to him as a gift by his brother, who had purchased the animal from a beggar for 2,000 toumans at the warfront near Iraq. He brought it here on the bus, in a crate tied up with rope. I don't know why Attah thought I would want the creature—perhaps he thought it would impress me that he had gotten his hands on something so exotic.

"At first we thought it would be good fun to have the baboon. Farideh even sewed a suit of clothes for it, thinking that it could be an amusing pet. But it was not a docile animal—far from it. It arrived here in an agitated, almost crazed state. As soon as the crate was opened, the animal sprang forward, hissing and clawing. It ran straight toward the orchard and climbed a tree, and there it stayed. For the first few weeks, it seemed to be adjusting well. We would spot it from the balcony, sometimes far away and sometimes nearby. On occasion when we walked through the orchards, we would see it huddled over the fruit that had fallen to the ground, jealously guarding its meal. We were a bit frightened by the way it appeared and disappeared, but it kept to itself and seemed completely uninterested in us."

Pedar-jaan pauses to load the opium pipe again and takes several hits. Then he looks at Andrew with an expression that is a mixture of curiosity and amusement, clears his throat again, and continues.

"As time went by, we would see the baboon less and less—only an occasional glimpse of its body jumping from tree to tree. But then, the creature began to show up more frequently. Once when we were having our tea on the balcony, it suddenly appeared over the railing, baring its teeth and demanding attention. We were shocked and frightened, and we all ran inside the house. I came back a few minutes later with a heaping plate of food—dried bread crusts, apples, leftover rice, whatever I could find. The animal promptly devoured my offering before it leapt over the balcony again and disappeared."

Pedar-jaan stops speaking abruptly and reaches again for the opium pipe. He motions for Andrew to come forward again and extends the pipe in his direction. Roya can hear the opium bubbling on the pipe and the sound of Andrew's breathing as he inhales the smoke. The night itself seems to be paused as the opium works its ancient spell on her husband. She translates as accurately as she can while her grandfather describes the baboon's repeated acts of violence in the bagh and the terror he and Farideh felt knowing that the creature was just outside their window when they fell asleep at night. Although the story he is telling is far from humorous, every time Roya looks at her grandfather, she notices that there is a touch of mirth on his face.

"One afternoon, Farideh was in the garden when the baboon came out of nowhere, lunged at her, and bit her on the leg, drawing blood. After this incident, I ordered the servants to find the baboon and chain it up. They dutifully did so, putting a collar around it and chaining it to a tree. It stayed there for several weeks, and I almost started to feel sorry for it.

"But then the baboon struck again, this time biting the gardener's five-year-old son, who had unknowingly come within the radius of its chain. I went down to the orchard where the incident had occurred, and found the bloody child hunched over with his arms crossed over his stomach, trying to stanch the blood that flowed from a spot on his abdomen and was seeping through his shirt. The baboon, still chained up, was emitting vicious growls from beneath its tree. I knew right then that it had to be done away with. If I'd had a weapon with me, I would have killed the creature myself.

"I summoned the workers and told them, in no uncertain terms, that they had to kill the baboon. They threw a gunny sack over the beast, tied it tightly, and beat the sack ferociously with sticks until it was stained with blood and the animal was silent. Then they brought the bloody sack to the entrance of the house and left it there. Even though the sack was still, I couldn't help feeling apprehensive as I stared at it. Dead or alive, I was afraid to be alone with the creature, so I turned and went inside the house. When I came out again a few hours later, the sack was still lying there, but it was empty."

The story hangs in the air while Pedar-jaan pauses to pour himself a cup of tea and sip it slowly. When his voice starts up again, his lilting Farsi sounds like music, and Roya senses that she is no longer a translator but instead has become some kind of medium, as if the words Andrew is absorbing were coming to him without her intervention, directly from Pedar-jaan himself.

"A few days later, Attah came to the house with the baboon's limp body in his arms. It had been hiding in the stables, and Attah had grabbed it by the foot, seized a shovel, and beaten it until it was lifeless. Again he placed the body on the ground at my feet, and again I am ashamed to admit that I was afraid. The creature now seemed to me to be something from another world, capable of eluding death. I ordered the men to build a box to bury the baboon in, and they came back an hour later with a coffin-shaped box made of wood. They placed the dead baboon inside it, nailed it shut, and put it in the back of the jeep. They later told me that they had placed the coffin inside of a dry well and had covered it with heavy stones. This time even the devil himself would not have been able to escape."

The story now appears to be over, and Pedar-jaan and Roya stop talking almost in unison. Andrew is staring at Pedar-jaan, open-mouthed, and Roya can't tell if he is shocked, frightened, or confused. He looks at her, then back at the old man.

"What an incredible story!" Andrew says this in English, not to Roya but to Pedar-jaan.

The old man stares at Andrew and chuckles softly. "*Saabr-kon. Dastaan tamaam na-shod.*" Roya does not need to translate because her husband has understood the Farsi: "Be patient. The story is not finished."

"Maybe the animal was the devil. The next morning the box was lying, splintered and empty, at the edge of the well. The baboon, of course, was nowhere to be seen. For several weeks the animal was spotted repeatedly, sometimes in one neighboring village and sometimes in another. I don't know how they did it, but the villagers finally managed to catch the creature again. They shot it with my hunting rifle, a direct shot in the temple."

This time when Pedar-jaan stops speaking, Andrew does not react. Pedar-jaan looks straight at him and fixes him in a stare, then utters the final line of the story—a line that Roya can find no way to soften.

"Then Attah beheaded the horrible creature. Or so I am told. I did not want to watch the execution."

Roya looks at the smile that is flickering across her grandfather's face, and her mind is suddenly flooded with a memory of another time she saw this smile. One summer as a child she had gone to the bagh with a Barbie doll her mother found for her on the black market. Pedar-jaan had picked the doll up and examined it with fascination. Watching her grandfather turn Barbie over in his hands, it suddenly occurred to Roya that the doll had breasts and was vaguely obscene. It astonished her that she had never noticed this before.

"I see that she is a woman," Pedar-jaan had said with a chortle. "I know she is from Amreeka, but here in Iran she must wear a hijab." He picked up a napkin from the table and wrapped it around Barbie's head. "Now she is Khaleh-Roghieh," he said. This was the name of the snaggle-toothed villager who baked their bread, a woman Roya had always been a bit frightened of.

Even as a child, Roya had known somewhere inside her that Pedar-jaan was teasing her and that his teasing was laced with love. But this was the moment when she first recognized her grandfather's ability to use a playful story the way others might use a knife. He has done that again tonight with the story of the baboon.

She can't formulate the exact message that her grandfather has delivered to her husband through the story, but she knows it has something to do with the assumptions Pedar-jaan thinks Andrew is making about Iran. In her mind, she conjures an image of the Muslims as they are depicted in the nightly newscasts she and Andrew watch in their living room in Atlanta: a dark mass of vicious animals who revel in violence and who must be contained. This image is immediately followed in her mind by a scene of human carnage, the aftermath of a drone strike on a nameless village.

She looks at her husband and sees the dazed expression that is frozen on his face, and she suddenly feels miles away from him. For an instant Andrew's physical appearance almost repulses her. His skin looks pallid, as though it were devoid of pigment. His hair has shaken loose and now looks scraggly, and his movements are awkward and vulgar as he lifts the glass of araq to his lips and swigs it all down at once. She hopes he will not speak because she does not want to hear his voice—not here, not now, not on this balcony.

A moth lands on Andrew's shoulder, and Pedar-jaan reaches over and brushes it off.

෩

After they are all in bed, the generator goes off, the moths disappear, and the bagh is once again enveloped in deep night. From the window of the bedroom where she and Andrew lie huddled together under a quilt, Roya can make out whole constellations of stars. The opium is still tingling in her veins, and she is alive with sensations. Just as she is beginning to give herself over to them, Andrew turns toward her and props himself up on his elbows.

"So, obviously, that story wasn't true, right?"

"How should I know? I didn't live here when it happened, remember?" She is surprised by the sharpness she hears in her own tone.

"I mean, your grandfather seems like a bit of a jokester. I think he might have been pulling my leg."

"Stop overthinking it, Andrew. It's just a story."

She turns away from him toward the wall, and they lie in silence for a while. Roya waits for the slow, deep breathing that indicates Andrew is asleep, but it does not come. He reaches for her shoulders in the dark, eases her over, and pulls her toward his chest. His body, which she knows is muscular and firm, suddenly seems to be made of rubber. She wonders if the opium is distorting her perceptions.

When he speaks, his voice sounds nasal and thin. "Hey, what do you think about making a baby tonight? Wouldn't it be cool to conceive a child here in Pedar-jaan's house?"

He tries his best to pronounce the name correctly, but he fails to roll the "r" and the "a" sounds come out dull and flat; unmistakably American. Roya stiffens. She had been ready for the opium initiation, but she is not ready to have sex in her family's bagh, in the bed she slept in as a child, with a man who can't pronounce her grandfather's name.

"No, Andrew, it wouldn't be cool at all. Let's just go to sleep."

"Okay, azizam," Andrew says, once again badly mangling the Farsi despite his best efforts to pronounce it carefully. Roya can't make out his face in the dark, but she can hear the gaiety in his voice. This is all great fun to him.

He kisses her softly on the cheek, and even when she turns her back to him again, he continues to hold her tightly. She tries to relax her body against his, but she is focused on the stars beyond the window. At first they seem distant, but after she stares at them for a while she begins to feel herself swimming among them, far away from her husband.

When she knows that Andrew has fallen asleep, Roya trains her ears toward the sounds of the night: the whir of bats' wings, the distant song of owls and bulbuls, the soft whoosh of the wind brushing against the trees. Then come the smells. A faint odor of opium is still lingering in the air, but now there are other aromas she has not noticed before: the smell of the desert dust lifting in the night breeze, the sweet perfume of the ripening cherries and grapes from the orchard below, the pungent odor of fresh sheep droppings from the mountains miles away.

As she closes her eyes and surrenders her body to sleep, she sees the face of her grandfather silhouetted against the stars and replays the sound of his ancient voice, telling a story she knows was not entirely true.

AZADI

RAANA'S APARTMENT WAS SMALL, and when her father, who was a tall man, entered it for the first time, it seemed even smaller. Mr. Alizadeh wasn't trying to be imposing. In fact, in the five hours he had been in her apartment Raana had been astonished by his attempts to behave the way he thought an American father might behave: he offered to make his own tea, asked if she needed help with dinner, and even helped to set the table. Mahin, Raana's mother, turned and looked at her husband several times during the course of the evening as though he had suddenly sprouted horns.

The day had been agonizing for Raana. It wasn't just the anticipation of seeing her parents after three years and having them in her new apartment for the very first time. It was the fact that she had become someone else altogether since they had last visited. She had become a full-fledged adult—a tax-paying member of society with a stable job and a gym membership. The longer she lived in the United States, the less her parents knew about her. All day long Raana had been feeling like she didn't know herself either, like an alien being had inhabited her body.

She had spent the entire morning chopping walnuts and squeezing fresh pomegranates to make fesenjun, which was one of the trickiest Persian dishes to make. She had never made it before, and she had gone into the kitchen at ten-minute intervals throughout the day to check the sauce like a neurotic housewife. She tasted the fesenjun so many times that its odor had permeated her skin.

She had already resolved that as soon as dinner was over, she would tell her parents about Abe. Both parents complimented her fesenjun, and while they ate, they told her about their flight and filled her in with news of Iran. She thought they would sit together in the living room after the dishes were cleared, but her mother went upstairs to unpack the suitcases. Raana could not tell her father about Abe without her mother present; it was uncomfortable enough just being alone with him for such a long period of time. She asked him if he wanted an after-dinner drink, and he asked for a glass of vodka with lime juice. She was careful to prepare his drink just the way he liked it: the vodka poured over two cubes of ice, no water, and both halves of the lime plopped into the glass. She brought it out to him and sat down beside him on the couch.

It was difficult for Raana to initiate a conversation with her father. His opinions on most matters were strong, and she always worried she would start an argument. She was thankful when he began talking, asking her a series of practical questions she could answer easily: How was her job? What was her neighborhood like? Where was the nearest grocery store?

When her father pulled a pack of cigarettes from his pocket, extracted a cigarette from it, and threw the pack on the coffee table, Raana picked it up and studied the cover.

"Azadi," she said. "Freedom. That's kind of an odd name for cigarettes, don't you think?"

"Yes. A lot of things are called Azadi in Iran now, ever since the Revolution, and all of them are ridiculous. The university near our house is called Azadi, although the women who go there must wear the full hijab and there are lots of restrictions on what students can study. There's Azadi Stadium, which was called Aryamehr Stadium when it was built by the Shah. Aryamehr means 'light of the Aryans' and was the made-up title the Shah gave himself. Ironic, isn't it? The best one is Azadi Tower, which is the new name for the old Sha-hyad Monument, Tehran's iconic landmark that the Shah built for his absurd celebration to mark the 2,500th anniversary of the Persian Empire. Very funny that it's called 'Freedom Tower' now, because the Shah's army killed lots of protesters there during the Revolution, and today the Pasdar and the Gasht-e-Ershad patrol it at all times of day and night looking for people to arrest. But here in America every-one likes the word 'freedom' too, and sometimes it is also applied to things that aren't exactly free. Don't you agree?"

"I guess so. But it's not the name I'm worried about, Baba-joon. It's what's inside the cigarettes."

"Do you think Winston and Marlboro are any better just be-cause they have shinier packaging? At least they don't spray pesticides on our tobacco in Iran. Of course, every now and then I do find a piece of plastic rolled inside one of my cigarettes."

"Baba, that's not funny. When was the last time you went to a doctor?"

"*Azizam*, I'm going to live as long as I am meant to live. Let me have my pleasures while I'm alive. Now that I'm retired, there's not much for me to do besides smoke. Anyway, with the air in Tehran being as polluted as it is, I'm probably better off inhaling cigarette smoke. It will filter out the car exhaust and the other fumes."

"I'm not trying to interfere in your life, Baba-joon. I just want you to be healthy, that's all."

When Raana's mother came back into the living room, she put her hand gently on her husband's head and said, "Come on, Navid. We need to go and sleep off our jet lag. We've been traveling for thirty-four hours."

Telling them about Abe would have to wait until tomorrow.

၎

She had met Abe a few months ago when they had both starred in the
local Town and Gown Theatre's production of *Jesus Christ Superstar*,
Raana as Mary Magdalene and Abe as Judas. Although she was a
decent singer and her alto voice was just in the right range for Mary
Magdalene's songs, she knew she had been chosen mostly because of
her long dark hair and her olive complexion. As much as she hated
to admit it, she knew she also shared a few personality traits with the
biblical Mary—before the demons were driven out of her. They had
the same basic dichotomy in their characters: tough on the outside
but vulnerable on the inside; domestically inclined but fiercely independent; part nurturer and part loose woman. All in all, she was right
for the role. But to cast an Iranian in a musical that paid homage to
the dawn of the Christian era seemed almost like a joke, especially
against the backdrop of the War on Terror.

As for Abe, he was perfect for the part of Judas in all the practical
ways. To begin with, he had the most astonishing singing voice Raana
had ever heard. The first time she heard him belting out "Heaven on
Their Minds" in rehearsal, she was spellbound. He was also the physical embodiment of the Judas character: dark and brooding, with a
chiseled face and a head full of chestnut-colored curls. The director
insisted that he perform "Damned for All Time" wearing nothing
but a tattered loincloth, and every time Raana watched him rehearse
the song, she had a hard time taking her eyes off him. He was lithe
and a little bit boyish, with angular shoulders and muscles that were
healthily but not excessively toned. He moved like some kind of wild
cat, in a graceful but calculated way. Watching him made Raana's
stomach flutter and her palms sweat.

Abe was also a Jew by birth, a fact that he shamelessly played up
when he auditioned for the part of Judas. And then, in an abrupt

about-face, he pointedly announced to Raana during their first conversation that he was a hardcore atheist. Every time she heard him sing the reprise of "I Don't Know How to Love Him" after that confession, she wanted to laugh out loud at the understatement.

The irony of Raana and Abe's casting wasn't lost on either of them; in fact, the catalyst for their first hookup was precisely their mutual recognition of that irony. It happened one night after rehearsal when the cast members all went out for drinks and she and Abe found themselves seated next to each other at the bar.

"So," he said as he clinked his glass of bourbon against hers, "I wonder what God thinks about a lapsed Jew from Georgia playing the part of Judas?"

"I wouldn't know," she said. "I'm more curious what Allah thinks about a Muslim woman from Iran playing Jesus's prostitute lover."

"Yeah, good question. Do you think those two are buddies up there? You think they agree on shit like that? Or maybe he's the same guy with some serious identity issues?"

"Or maybe he's not a guy at all. Why is it that you Americans, even if you're not Christian, always imagine God as looking like an American man—like a huge John Wayne sitting up in the clouds? I mean, must you always be so literal? Why don't people have more imagination?"

Abe chortled. "Or maybe he—or she, or it—doesn't exist at all. Are you non-literal enough to imagine that?"

They opened their eyes at the same time the next morning and lay in silence for several minutes watching the intermittent flicker of the commuters' headlights blinking in through the venetian blinds. They could hear the muffled sounds of car engines in the distance, mixed with the more immediate sound of morning birds chirping from the tree outside the bedroom window. Raana was slightly hung over and could tell Abe was too. It felt momentous to be waking up next to him, but she decided to make light of it.

"So, what happened last night? Did you take advantage of me when I was under the influence? Do I still have my virtue?"

"Which virtue would that be? You seem to have so many! One of them, I'm told, is that you make a killer bacon-and-egg breakfast."

"That's pretty cheeky for someone who barely knows me. Besides, neither one of us is supposed to eat pork. You, Jew, me, Muslim. Hello?"

"According to which one of those men in the sky? Could it be the same one who says we shouldn't sleep together without clearing it with the government first? Or maybe it's the one who says we have to convert each other if we're even going to date? You convert to Judaism, and I'll convert to Islam. Oh, wait…"

When she looked at him and saw the mischief in his eyes, she knew she had fallen for him.

℀

On the morning of his second day in his daughter's apartment, Mr. Alizadeh was craving what he liked to call a "cowboy" breakfast: bacon, eggs, hashbrowns, toast. He was fond of classic Westerns and adored the whole Western aesthetic, which had always baffled Raana. Her father's style, as she remembered it, featured European tailored suits with tapered waists, immaculately pressed shirts, and expensive shoes—the kind of clothing many Americans, especially cowboys, would have thought effeminate. She sometimes wondered whether her father's obsession with cowboys was another one of his sardonic mind games. But it occurred to her that maybe there was something about the cowboy life—the ruggedness, the open land sweeping up toward distant mountains, the campfires at night—that reminded him of his childhood in Iran.

More than the food, her father loved the ritual of preparing a sumptuous meal in the morning and eating it in a leisurely fashion.

During the years when he was working in a government office in Tehran, he often had to eat breakfast in a hurry, grabbing a piece of naan and *paneer* and downing it quickly with chai before rushing off to fight the traffic. A big American breakfast seemed like a reward for a life of hard work.

There was no bacon in the refrigerator, so Raana offered to go to the Super-Walmart down the street to buy some. Her father immediately offered to go with her. He loved shopping in the United States and loved shopping at Walmart most of all. Raana usually avoided big box stores altogether, and she dreaded the thought of going to Walmart with him. He would want to wander down every aisle to study the items on display. He was especially fascinated by gadgetry: bag sealers, jar openers, knife sharpeners, and other such items that didn't exist in Iran. A trip to Walmart with her father meant hours in the housewares section of the store.

They arrived at the store at about eight forty-five, and by the time they left, it was almost eleven. Today's Walmart expedition yielded an LED flashlight, an electronic key finder, a large bag of disposable razors, a battery charger, a package of boxer shorts, two pairs of jeans, a flannel shirt, and a cheap "ten-gallon" cowboy hat made of imitation straw. He didn't intend to really wear the hat, he told Raana, but he thought it would be amusing to his friends back home.

"We can have the bacon tomorrow," Mr. Alizadeh said in the checkout line. "It's time for lunch now. How about we pick up your mother and I treat the two of you to McDonald's?"

Raana wanted to remind her father that she didn't eat fast food, but she knew he would somehow manage to talk her into it. She could have a salad.

"Whatever you want to do, Baba-joon."

The tight booth and red and yellow colors of McDonald's didn't seem like the appropriate atmosphere for telling her parents about

Abe, so she decided to wait until the afternoon. She knew that when they got home her father would want his nap. The afternoon nap was a sacred tradition to Navid Alizadeh. Even in the years when he had only a tiny window of free time when he came home at midday, he insisted on putting on his pajamas and closing his eyes, claiming that even a few minutes of sleep would restore him.

He did not put on his pajamas this afternoon, but instead slept fully clothed in the new jeans he had bought at Walmart. Raana could hear him snoring loudly from the bedroom. He slept for two full hours and was in a good mood when he woke up. It was a pleasant afternoon, so they decided to sit on the back patio of the apartment to have their afternoon tea. Navid drank two cups of black tea and smoked four cigarettes.

Her father's good mood wasn't going to last forever, Raana thought, so it was now or never.

When she was rehearsing how she would present her relationship with Abe to her parents, it had dawned on her that the Farsi word *eyb*, which meant "defect," was pronounced exactly the same as Abe's name. She decided she would preempt the inevitable jokes by avoiding the nickname altogether, and instead telling her parents his name was Ibrahim. The name was common among both Muslims and Jews, and it was, after all, his real name.

"My friend Ibrahim is coming over this evening to meet you," she said. Then she added, "He is my boyfriend, actually."

"Is he Jewish?" Mr. Alizadeh asked immediately.

"Yes," Raana said. She wanted to ask, "So what?" but she stopped herself.

"What does he do?"

"He is training to be an actor."

"It doesn't matter that he is Jewish," her father said. "But the lack of job—that matters, Raana-joon. You don't want to have to support your husband, do you?"

"First of all, he's not my husband, and probably never will be. Secondly, he has a job. Two jobs, in fact. He's actually supporting *me* right now." This was true. Abe was working as a tutor on weekends and performing at the Shakespeare Tavern six nights a week, all while finishing his degree.

"Do you need some money, azizam?" Offering money was always Navid Alizadeh's way of circumventing difficult conversations with his daughter.

Raana tried to hide her exasperation. "No, Baba-joon, I'm fine. I have a full-time teaching job, remember?"

Raana knew that her job as a fifth-grade teacher was not respectable in her father's eyes. Abe's acting career was even more shameful—she might as well have told her father that he was a thief. She was reminded of the great chain of being popular in Medieval times, where everything in the universe, from mollusks to angels, was rank-ordered.

Abe was on his best behavior when he showed up that evening. He arrived at the door in a clean polo shirt and khaki trousers, a bottle of expensive whiskey and a bouquet of flowers in his hand. Raana ushered him out to the patio, where the kabab that Mahin had made earlier was cooking on the grill. After the introductions, Mr. Alizadeh poured a whiskey for himself and another for Abe. He sat down in a chair facing Abe and looked at him with a smile.

"So, I'm told you want to go to Hollywood to become an actor?"

"I don't have such big dreams, Mr. Alizadeh," Abe responded, pronouncing the surname perfectly. "There are other ways to make money in acting. Too much competition in Hollywood."

"There are many Jewish people in Hollywood, correct? I've heard that the whole place is run by Jews."

"I really don't know much about who runs Hollywood," Abe said. "I've never been there."

Raana had known her father would not be able to avoid bringing the conversation around to Abe's Jewish heritage. She would try to steer him elsewhere, although she knew it was a lost cause. "Baba-joon, why don't you ask Abe about what he studied in school?" she said. "He has a degree in history, which should interest you, since you are a scholar."

"Oh, then, he should know about the history of the Jews in Iran. Did you know, Ibrahim, that Cyrus the Great actually freed the Jews who were enslaved in Babylon in the sixth century BC? I'm sure you know that he was the greatest leader of the Persian Empire. We revere him in my country."

"No, I didn't know that. Interesting."

"When I was growing up, there were many, many Jews in Iran. They had thriving businesses. I had Mahin's wedding ring made by a Jewish goldsmith."

Raana looked at Abe and could tell he was faltering for something to say in response. But her father didn't give him a chance to formulate his thoughts.

"Muslims are not the way your media depicts them," Mr. Aliza-deh continued. "We are tolerant people. We respect all people of the book. And by the way, we recognize that *your* book—your Torah—is older than ours by many centuries."

Raana had known her father would deliver this narrative; she had heard it countless times before. He was not a religious man, and he wasn't really anti-Semitic either. But like most Iranians, he couldn't shake the ingrained notion that ethnicity was a core part of a person's identity. Fortunately, she had prepared Abe for her father's little discourse on Judaism, and he didn't appear to be offended.

"I was just a child when the state of Israel was founded," Navid went on, "but I was taught to respect what the Jews had made out of nothingness, in the middle of the desert. I have a lot of respect for your people. You must not blame me for the attitude of my government towards your people. I do not share that attitude."

Raana was surprised by Abe's answer. "I won't," he said, "if you won't blame me for mine. I didn't elect Netanyahu."

"Of course you didn't! And I'm guessing that you didn't vote for Trump either. I don't know which of the two is more diabolical, but I fear for the world with those two in power. They are criminals."

"I couldn't agree more," Abe said, his face brightening. On the topic of Trump, Abe was fully in his element. But Navid was still determined to steer the conversation.

"Trump is not consistent. On the one hand he makes hateful comments about the Jews and encourages the neo-Nazis, and on the other hand he allies himself with Netanyahu. This is because the two men hate the Muslims and will do whatever they can to punish us. And believe me, the people of Iran are suffering under Trump's sanctions, which of course are applauded by Netanyahu. Children are dying because of the lack of medicine, just like they did in Iraq. It is not the children's fault, I'm sure you will agree."

Raana wanted to interrupt her father; to tell him that it was unfair for him to classify Abe as both a Jew and an American, responsible for the actions of both governments. It seemed especially unfair because Abe had no allegiance whatsoever to country or ethnicity; he shunned all labels and called himself a member of the "human family." Mahin called them to dinner before Raana could come to his defense.

Over dinner, Abe asked Mr. Alizadeh many questions about Iran, all of them well informed and carefully formulated. He avoided direct mentions of politics and instead focused on issues he knew he and Raana's father would agree on: health care, the refugee crisis, wealth distribution. He had read a great deal about the underground scene in Iran—the rampant prostitution and heroin and methamphetamine addiction; the wild raves that were held in secret locations all over the city; the Gatsby-like parties thrown in the mansions of northern Tehran. When he asked Raana's father about these dimensions of Iran, Navid frowned and nodded his head. "You are right," he said. "These excesses are worse than they were in the Shah's day."

Raana felt tense. At any moment, the conversation could veer into dangerous territory. She suggested watching a movie, but her father didn't want to. "I am enjoying the conversation," he said, "and the night air is very pleasant." Raana knew what he was really enjoying was smoking and drinking so freely, which he could not do in the Islamic Republic.

Raana lost count of how many cigarettes her father smoked and how many whiskeys he drank. When the pack of cigarettes was almost gone and the bottle of whiskey almost finished, Navid Alizadeh got up and left the patio.

It was not his wife, or even his daughter, who noticed how long he was gone. It was Abe.

It was Abe who went inside, walked toward the bathroom, and pushed the door open.

It was Abe who picked Navid's limp body off the floor.

It was Abe who called 911.

It was Abe who explained to the paramedic what Mr. Alizadeh had eaten for dinner, how many whiskeys he had consumed, and how many cigarettes he had smoked.

And when Navid Alizadeh awoke from his emergency bypass surgery and looked at the faces of his daughter and his wife, the first words out of his mouth were, "Where is Ibrahim?"

HER REVOLUTION

S HIREEN'S OFFICE WAS ON the east side of the campus, and at certain times of day sunlight flooded in through its two large windows. From one of the windows, she could see the green expanse of the football field, always perfectly groomed, and the state-of-the-art science building that had been built last year thanks to a million-dollar donation by one of the school's high-profile alumni. But it was the other view—the one from the window right above her desk—that Shireen was always drawn to. Just beyond the window was a grassy area with benches arranged daintily beneath a towering magnolia tree.

After so many years of looking out at this tree, Shireen had developed a kinship with it. It had been there since the school was established in the 1950s, and she calculated it to be about her own age. In the winter months, when Shireen was feeling trapped and restless, its craggy profile against the gray sky provided a touch of beauty. In spring it offered up fragrant flowers that looked like open parasols, giving her a burst of optimism.

The name inscribed on the door of her office read SHIREEN MOGHADDAS, but she insisted that her students call her Ms. M. Their mouths contorted in odd ways when they tried to pronounce her last name, and it always came out sounding vaguely obscene. Her students were free to visit her whenever she was in her office, but she usually kept the door firmly closed. Lately she was seeking refuge in her office more frequently, slipping inside for a few minutes in the middle of a lesson while her students were doing group work, and even taking her lunch there. Shireen had never cared for the small talk in the cafeteria, but now, after thirteen years at the school, she found it almost impossible to bear. She couldn't decide which was worse: the overzealous novice teachers who still thought they had the power to change society with their half-baked ideas, or the jaded "lifers" who seemed to do nothing but complain. Shireen's age and tenure would place her in this latter camp, but she didn't have much in common with them, and sensed that they found her a bit odd.

On this day in early November, she ducked into her office the moment her tenth-grade Honors group left the classroom and quickly closed the door behind her. She had fifty-five minutes until her next class, and she needed to detox. She poured herself a cup of coffee and sat down in the swivel chair in front of her desk. The computer was blinking at her, but she couldn't face her school email right away. Instead, she sipped her coffee and stared out the window at the magnolia tree. A few students she didn't recognize were sitting on the benches beneath it, some with books open on their knees and others holding animated conversations she couldn't hear through the window. Behind them, other students were passing purposefully through the quad on their way to class. She remained fixated on the scene for some time, lost in thought.

Turning back toward her computer, she decided to scroll through *Iran Primer*, a website from the United States Institute of Peace that covered news from Iran. Shireen went to this website at least once a day, even though most of what she read there depressed her. Today's articles were especially unpleasant: a U.N. report on human rights violations in Iran; an opinion piece on whether the Iran nuclear deal could be resuscitated; an update on Iran's morality police and the enforcement of the hijab. The heavy content of the website was a bit too much for her today, but it was better than answering school emails, so she perused.

When she had less than fifteen minutes left before class, she shut the website down and clicked on the envelope icon at the bottom of her page to open her personal email.

There were three messages. The first was from her mother in Iran; a status report on her recovery from knee replacement surgery. The second was from her health club offering her a free facial. She read through both of these emails absently, then clicked on the third, which was from an address she didn't recognize. It was a five-line email typed in a tiny font:

Dear Shireen,

I found your email address on the Internet. 35 years is a long time, and many things have happened in our lives since then. I don't know if you want to hear from me, but I thought I would tell you that I am well. I have been out of Evin for more than 20 years. I got my papers, and I am now living in Germany. You are many miles away, but I feel you are close. I have felt you close for all this time. I will hope for an answer from you.

Your friend, Ahmad

She rubbed her eyes, took a sip of her coffee, and read the note again—and then a third time and a fourth. She didn't need a last name to identify the writer: Ahmad Rastegar, a man she had not seen or heard from since she was eighteen. There was nothing in the email's appearance or content to make her doubt its authenticity. She leaned in toward the screen and examined the email more closely, as though Ahmad himself might be hiding within the lines. After reading it a few more times, she scribbled the address on a scrap of paper, folded the paper up, and placed it in her wallet behind her driver's license. Then she deleted the email.

She swiveled her chair toward the window and stared out at the magnolia tree, which suddenly looked like an impressionist painting. When a knock came on her office door, it took her a moment to remember where she was.

"Ms. M! You in there? You planning to teach us today?" The voice belonged to Ryan Chestnut, one of the seniors from her AP Literature class. She looked at the clock: her next lesson was supposed to have started six minutes ago.

"I'll be right in, Ryan. Just finishing up something in here."

Like most veteran teachers, Shireen had good days and bad days in the classroom—days when she was merely going through the motions and days when she had sudden bursts of inspiration. She still felt passionate about most of the books she taught, and on her good days she managed to transmit this passion to her students. But over the course of her long teaching career, it had become harder and harder for her to convince students of the value of studying literature. Even when she jazzed up her lessons with YouTube videos and hands-on projects of questionable pedagogical value, her students rolled their eyes, sighed heavily, and made comments like "It's soooo boring!" about books like *Song of Solomon* and *Native Son*—anything that was more than half an inch thick and had a modicum of philosophical content. Sometimes her students' perspectives on the classics were amusing. Once while she was teaching *Pride and Prejudice*, a student had blurted out, "I wish he would just *kiss* her already!" and Shireen had to grudgingly agree that the girl had a point. But it troubled her that her students could no longer handle prose with an average sentence length of more than six words. Her colleagues called her a purist and a philistine, but she didn't care. She wasn't about to add *The Hunger Games* to her curriculum.

Even though they attended one of the most expensive private schools on the East Coast, Shireen sometimes thought of her students as underprivileged. The school was founded right after *Brown v. Board of Education*, and it was no secret that it had been a "white flight" school. Although its brochures and yearbook covers always featured a token person of color, the bleachers during football games were still a ribbon of white. These kids had been born inside a thick cocoon, and Shireen was on a mission to break through it.

Today's class was supposed to focus on *Madame Bovary*. She had a sudden vision for the lesson as she got up from her swivel chair and entered the classroom. Instead of discussing the realism, the nuances, and the hidden details the book was known for, she would discuss the relative virtue of its heroine.

"So, let's see a show of hands," she said as soon as she was in front of the classroom. "How many in here think Emma should be condemned for her actions?"

Her students looked at her with mute faces. She rephrased the question.

"How many think it's acceptable for a married woman to have affairs just because she's bored with her middle-class existence or because she craves sensual pleasure?"

The hands shot up.

The discussion soon digressed into a comparison of Emma Bovary with the other female protagonists the students knew: Lady Macbeth, Cleopatra, Hester Prynne, Daisy Buchanan. Shireen, still in the thrall of her vision, posed another question.

"Why is it that there are no female protagonists who are middle-aged? Can anyone think of one? There are lots of grandmothers, widows, lonely and disabled elderly women—but where are the middle-aged women? They seem to be the 'tweens' of the adult world, the invisible generation. Everyone assumes that they are past their sexual prime, and that they have no libido, no ambition—nothing of interest to offer."

"What about Penelope?" This came from Laura Vale, the top student in the class. "She has to be middle-aged, right?"

Shireen considered this answer for a moment. "Okay, Laura, let's calculate her age. Even though she has a twenty-year-old son when the epic opens, women had children early back then, so that probably makes her under forty. She was nineteen or twenty when Odysseus left for the Trojan War, and he's gone for twenty years. Again, that makes her about forty. Everyone assumes that a forty-year-old is still desirable, and Penelope obviously is, because she spends most of those twenty years surrounded by eligible bachelors who are desperate to marry her. But she stays faithful to Odysseus even when he's sleeping with women all over the Mediterranean. So, she's not exactly middle-aged, and she's hardly an example of a strong, independent woman."

Shireen looked out over her classroom at her immaculate students, the boys in their pressed khaki trousers with their long legs slightly spread, the girls in their blue skirts with their ankles primly crossed beneath their desks. At the back of the classroom, Wade Boylan was raising his hand. Even though he was on the basketball team and generally considered to be of the "jock" persuasion, he was an astute young man, and Shireen liked him. But there was something about him—a certain cockiness and an impertinence—that unsettled her.

"What do you think, Wade?"

"Well, if all women your age were as hot as you, Ms. M., maybe there would be more of them in novels."

"Flattery will get you nowhere," Shireen said. "And that's not an answer to the question."

But it was exactly what she wanted to hear right now, as she conjured an image of Ahmad Rastegar in her mind.

∽

Shireen had met Ahmad on a beach, which was probably her first mistake. She should have known better. You didn't meet a man on a beach in the newly formed Islamic Republic—not when you were seventeen, not when you were a promising student with a bright future ahead of you, and not when you were from a respectable family who lived in north Tehran. If you happened to encounter a man and he approached you—even looked at you—you were to pretend that he was invisible, or that you were invisible, or that the encounter wasn't happening at all, or that an evil spirit of some sort was tempting you to forget the code of decency that had been etched in your mind at birth.

But Ahmad was there, and he was unaccompanied. The fact that he was alone on the beach should have been a warning sign, but it didn't feel like one. He was not parading his body or scouting around for a girl to pick up; he was trailing a stick through a patch of sand, circumscribing a small area that appeared to be of no particular interest. Shireen wasn't even sure he had spotted her. She looked up from the chair where she was sitting in front of her parents' villa, and there he was. She was fully clothed in her roopoosh and roosaree—the only way a woman could appear on a public beach in the Islamic Republic—but her headscarf was draped loosely over her head and shoulders. A textbook lay open in her lap, but she was not really concentrating on it.

From her vantage point a few meters away, Shireen watched in fascination as Ahmad bent his body at the waist and retrieved an object from inside the circle he had drawn. With the object clutched firmly in his hand, he moved toward her until he stood directly over her chair, looking down at her. Even when he was standing right there, she couldn't make out what he was holding. It was a curved object that seemed to have been polished and oiled, but it didn't resemble any object she had ever seen before.

"*Ajeeb-e, na?* It's odd, isn't it," he said, "to find something like this here, on the beach?" He thrust the object toward her in his open palm, like a waiter offering a drink on a tray, and she saw that it was a horn. She had no idea what kind of animal it might have belonged to. Perhaps a goat or a cow?

She was momentarily confused. A man she didn't know was offering her a bizarre gift, and a faint voice inside her told her she must not accept it. He looked to be about ten years older than she was, but the expression on his face was childlike and earnest. He had heavy eyebrows crowning deep-set eyes, and a light sprinkling of facial hair as though he had forgotten to shave today. It was obvious that he had dressed thoughtlessly. His thin body, clad in a tattered black sweater and Kurdish trousers, looked as fragile as the stick that was dangling from his hand.

It took several moments for the incongruity of a horn on the Caspian seashore to become evident to her, and she wasn't sure how she should answer his simple question. A response somehow pushed itself forward and escaped her lips.

"*Aareh, ye kami ajeeb-eh.* Yes, it is a little odd. Do you know what animal it comes from? And how it got here? How it ended up on the beach?"

"I think it's a ram's horn. I guess it's probably been here a while because it looks like it's been washed by the sea. Maybe a ram wandered away from a herd in one of the mountain villages and ended up here. It probably died on this beach."

Shireen knew he was suggesting that there was a buried meaning in this phenomenon, but she couldn't quite formulate the idea. From the angle where she was sitting, he was framed by a cloudburst shot through with the fading afternoon light and looked almost unreal. Behind him she could hear the gentle whoosh of the surf and the faint cawing of seabirds. She looked again at the outstretched hand that was holding the horn and noticed that his skin was taut and weathered, as though his bones were covered over with a thin layer of leather.

He thrust the horn in her direction, and she lifted it from his palm and began to examine it. But she did not have time to make a response before he seized it back from her, raised it to his lips, and blew on it. The sound was somehow ancient and tragic, like the cry of a mother giving birth.

∾

Back in Tehran one Friday when her parents were away at their villa, Shireen called the number Ahmad had scrawled on the inside cover of her book. The phone rang many times, and she ran her fingers over the ram's horn while she waited for him to answer. She was just about to hang up when she heard his voice saying *Allo?* on the other end.

"Ahmad, Salaam. Shireen hastam," she said. She started to remind him that she was the girl he had met on the beach a few weeks ago, but he didn't need the reminder. He responded immediately, cutting her short.

"Shireen! Khoda-ra-shokr! Thank God you called! I was sure that I had scared you and that I would never see you again. Where are you?"

"Alone at home. Should I come to you?"

Why was she so unafraid to go to the home of this man she didn't know? She had a notebook and pen ready, and she scribbled his address down. Immediately after she hung up, she picked up the phone again and called a telephone taxi.

It took the better part of an hour for her to reach his apartment. The taxi twisted through the streets of the labyrinthine part of downtown known as pa'een shahr, weaving in and out of traffic, dodging pedestrians and fruit stands. Shireen had lived in Tehran all her life, but never in her seventeen years had she ventured so far south. Because she had met Ahmad on a beach, without a clear backdrop or context, it hadn't occurred to her that he might live down here, beneath the cloud of smog she had seen from her parents' balcony. Even the trees seemed impoverished in this part of the city; their trunks were covered in grime and their leaves were curled up as if in self-defense. They were nothing like the stately trees in the north where she lived, which draped their leafy branches over the wide streets and shook them in the breeze like women loosening their hair.

The taxi dropped her in front of a small apartment building on the narrowest street she had ever been on. She rang the buzzer and Ahmad's voice came over the intercom.

"Aamadam pa'een. I'm on my way down."

At the door, Ahmad gave her a stiff nod, looked from side to side to make sure no one had seen a woman visiting him, then turned and led her up two flights of stairs and into his tiny apartment. There was a dark entryway that opened into two adjoining rooms separated by an embroidered curtain. In one of these rooms there was a small refrigerator, a countertop gas burner, a samovar, and a rickety table with two cane-backed chairs. The floor of the other room was covered from end to end with a carpet, worn but exquisitely beautiful. A small mattress was folded neatly in one corner with bedding arranged on top of it. In the other corner there was a squat shelf that was sagging from the weight of the books it held, and next to it sat several untidy piles of loose books, magazines, and newspapers.

Shireen removed her headscarf and her roopoosh, and Ahmad guided her to the wooden table and pulled a chair out for her. He seemed afraid to look at her at first, and when his hand glanced against hers as he served her tea, he quickly withdrew it. They sat at the table and spoke for a long time about a range of mundane subjects: their families, his frustrating job at the Ministry of Education, her plans to attend Tehran University in the fall, the places they had traveled and the places they wanted to travel. During a lull in the conversation Ahmad suddenly got up from the table, walked over to the bookshelf, and seized from it a book with a photograph of a woman on the cover.

"Have you read Forough?" he asked.

"No," she confessed. "I've heard her name, but I thought her books were illegal."

"They are. But they are also the greatest poems written in our language in the twentieth century. Like most banned books, they are important to read. It is our duty to read them."

At first, she feigned interest when Ahmad began to read the poems to her—but the more she listened, the more genuine her interest became. The combination of the words she was hearing, Ahmad's melodic voice, and the complex odors of the city blowing in through the open windows of the apartment gave her the heady sensation that an astronaut might feel when experiencing weightlessness for the first time.

Other than a few gentle brushes of his fingers against her arm or shoulder as he helped her put on her roopoosh later that afternoon, Ahmad did not touch Shireen's body that day. His focus was on touching her mind—and to that purpose, he sent her home with *Another Birth*, the book of poems he had been reading to her.

That night in bed, Shireen studied the cover photograph depicting the gorgeous poetess, then opened to the book's preface and learned the tragic story of Forough's life: her marriage to a second cousin at the tender age of sixteen, her daring extrication of herself from this marriage a few years later, the bohemian lifestyle she subsequently lived, and her horrifying death in an automobile accident when she was only thirty-two. She read *Another Birth* straight through, then read it again, dwelling on one passage from the title poem so many times that she committed it to memory:

> *In the garden I plant my hands*
> *I know I shall grow, I know, I know*
> *swallows will lay their eggs*
> *in the nest of my ink-stained fingers*
> *twin pairs of bright cherries*
> *will be my earrings*
> *and dahlia petals will dress my fingernails*

She hid the book in her nightstand beneath the ram's horn, like an addict hiding a secret stash, then turned the light off and fell asleep.

When her parents returned home the next day, she could not bear to look at them. Her mother shuffled through the house in her bedroom slippers, fretting about her upcoming dinner party. Her father sat in front of the television smoking cigarette after cigarette, shaking his head and cursing at the evening news. Neither of them seemed to have a clue that there were people like Ahmad down there under that cloud of smog—people who thought deeply, people who were gentle and hopeful, people who read books.

Shireen didn't have classes on Wednesday afternoons, so the following Wednesday she went to a phone booth down the street from her parents' apartment and called Ahmad again. He was alone and asked her to come. Without a moment's hesitation, she raced upstairs and told her parents that she was going to a friend's house to study, then went back down and called a telephone taxi. Again, after the tea and the conversation, Ahmad read to her, this time a passage from the Farsi translation of *The Jungle* which he had already marked and placed on the table before she arrived.

As she was leaving that afternoon, Ahmad stopped her and put his hand on her arm.

"I was thinking that perhaps you could come every Wednesday. We can read something new each time you come."

"I will come next Wednesday," Shireen said.

She told her parents that she had volunteered to tutor a friend on Wednesday afternoons, and over the next few months she visited Ahmad faithfully each week. Together they pored over the books that were on his shelf: Marx and Lenin, Dostoevsky, Sholokhov, Huxley, Thomas More. They only dared to see each other outside of his apartment on two occasions. The first was one Wednesday afternoon when they met beside the river in Darband, a village at the foot of the Alborz Mountains to the north of Tehran. Unmarried men and women were not allowed to be together in the Islamic Republic, but they told the owner of the restaurant that they were cousins, and he did not question them. They sat together on a wooden *takht* beside the river, speaking lightheartedly as they drank tea and ate kabab. At one point, Ahmad reached over and tucked a loose strand of Shireen's hair inside her hijab, a gesture that startled but thrilled her. It was the only time during those months that he ever made an attempt to touch her.

The second meeting outside of Ahmad's apartment took place in Shireen's neighborhood, a part of the city he had never been to. She had seen where he lived, she argued, so it was only fair that he should see where she lived. Ahmad was mostly silent as they walked together through the wide streets of northern Tehran. When she pointed out the building she lived in, a high-rise with gleaming one-way glass, he turned to her and spoke.

"You know, the mistake people make about us is that they think we want everyone to live the way I live. The point is for everyone to live like this." He swept his arm through the air toward the apartment building. "When the real revolution comes, that is what will happen."

This was the first inkling Shireen had that Ahmad might be involved in dangerous underground politics. The next indication came a few weeks later, when she arrived at his apartment to find him sitting at the wooden table holding his head in his hands, sobbing like a child. Shireen had never seen him in such an emotional state. She walked over to him and put her hand on his shoulder.

"Please tell me what has happened, Ahmad-joon. You know you can trust me."

"It is too awful to think about, let alone to speak about."

Gradually, she pulled the story out of him: his cousin Shahrzad, who was only twenty-two years old, had been executed the day before. Her crime, Shireen learned, was working for the underground network that helped the members of the Tudeh party—Marxist rebels opposed to Khomeini—to escape from Iran into Kurdistan.

"She was an angel, Shireen, an angel who never did anything wrong in her life. Those bastards killed her before she even had her first kiss. They shot her in the temple with a pistol, and then called my aunt and uncle after it was over to tell them to come and collect her body. They are *madar-sag*. Sons of dogs. They think that they have power just because they wear turbans on their heads, but they are wrong. They will pay."

 લ્જ

It was on a Wednesday afternoon many weeks later that everything between them changed. At first Shireen listened patiently while Ahmad read to her from *Anna Karenina*, smiling when he got to the charged scene in which Anna and Vronsky first discover their attraction for one another. When he paused to begin a new chapter, she suddenly reached across the table, seized the book from him, snapped it shut, and grasped his hands in her own. Then she looked straight into his face and told him, in no uncertain terms, that she wanted to become his lover.

Ahmad was too stunned to speak at first, but finally sputtered, *"Motma'en hastee?* Are you certain?" His face was so flushed that Shireen could almost feel heat rising from it.

She didn't hesitate before answering, "I am certain. *Meekhaamet.* I desire you."

Using his trademark logic, Ahmad laid out for her the possible consequences of this entanglement. His gallantry only made her want him more. She knew he responded well to sensible arguments, so she summoned all her rhetorical powers to convince him that the move was appropriate and just. She was fully aware of the risks of her decision, she said, but she knew that it was the right thing to do. She didn't consider it a loss of her virtue, but rather a logical next step in their relationship and in her formation as an independent woman.

"Ahmad-joon, we are soulmates, aren't we? I thought you were an atheist and a Marxist. Only backward Judeo-Christian thinking, with its concepts of sin and guilt, would regard the sexual union between two consenting partners as dirty and immoral, don't you agree? What about Forough? It was her sexuality that made her a rebel. Even Tolstoy, a Christian, understood that people need sex. That's what the passage you just read was all about."

"My mother and my aunts are the only women who have ever kissed me," he said.

To this she responded by rising from her chair, extending her hand toward his, and leading him into the bedroom, where she turned out the light, unfurled the mattress, and began unbuttoning her blouse.

His first caresses were tentative, and the wariness of his touch made it feel like soft breath on her skin. The mattress was thin beneath them, but she was buoyed by his arms encircling her and had the sensation of being surrounded by water or silk. She knew his frame was made of jutting bones, but as she touched them, they seemed to soften into clay. He was not clumsy or shy. But after the act was over, he leaned his forehead on her shoulder, and she could feel his body trembling.

Shireen's mother had instructed her in the rudiments of sexual intercourse and had warned her of the consequences, both moral and practical, of sex before marriage. But Shireen was not prepared for the imperious urges that she felt after she became Ahmad's lover. She developed a fascination with her own body, and she could not get enough of it. When she gazed at her naked figure before the mirror each night, everything about it excited her, from her rounded hips to her smooth, firm belly to the way her long hair black hair fell over her breasts. It gave her a thrill to imagine Ahmad's hands touching her.

She did not know how she had acquired her expertise, but somehow it happened that Ahmad became her eager apprentice, and she, nine years younger, became the intrepid explorer, leading him into undiscovered realms with a combination of patience and tender amusement. More than the feel of his firm body against hers, more even than the way he moved against her and whispered her name, it was his innocence that made him sublime.

ல

Shortly after this new phase of their relationship began, Shireen awoke one morning with a tangible hollowness in the innermost cavities of her body. The feeling was somehow familiar even though she could not have felt it before. It was a craving—almost a hunger—so profound that every part of her rang out with it. She had no scientific knowledge of the stages of gestation, but she felt the quickening almost from the start. Her senses recognized it. Each segment of her body, each minute part of her from the tips of her hair to the cells at her very core, pulsated. She sensed her insides opening up like ripe fruit, and when she touched her hands to her belly it felt as if she was reaching back in time and touching Ahmad, caressing the tiny being that he had once been, years before she herself was born.

In her bed at night, she was filled with crushing love for the universe and all that was in it. There was not a moment of guilt or remorse for what she had done—she was alive with moral righteousness and a sense of purpose that made her understand, for the first time, why she was alive. But when the light of day shone on her, the truth came crashing down: she had committed a capital crime, and if she did not hide the evidence of it she would put herself in grave danger. Even worse than that, she would put Ahmad in danger. She wanted the baby growing inside her so badly that she was ready to abandon father, mother, family, home, and country for it—but it simply could not be.

There was no other solution: she had to get rid of the child, and she had to do it alone. She would not tell Ahmad about her condition, nor would she share with him her devastating decision. She would go straight to Nader Hejazi, her mother's cousin who had recently returned from Iran with a medical degree from the United States. She didn't know Nader well, but she felt certain that he would not judge her or betray her. And so she called him one evening, just moments after feeling the first twinges of the most delicious nausea she had ever experienced.

It was not in Shireen's nature to be circumspect. She immediately blurted into the telephone, "Hello, Doctor Hejazi. This is Shireen. I need your help."

Nader did not have to ask her what kind of help she needed. There was no hint of a reprimand in his voice as he calmly instructed her to come to his office the following day. The procedure was illegal in the Islamic Republic, he explained, but it had been legal under the Shah, and he had the equipment in his clinic to take care of her problem. The Islamic government still allowed abortions when the mother's life was in danger. "I know your life isn't exactly in danger," he said, "but in a way I suppose it is."

She had a rush of panic when she arrived at the office the following evening, but once she was behind the heavy wooden doors of the office, she knew that she was safe. The curtains were drawn against the Tehran night, and it was almost eerily quiet. Flashes of car headlights could be seen intermittently through the fabric, but the sounds of the city were muffled. For a fleeting moment she felt as if she was viewing Tehran on a movie screen and that she was not actually present in the city—not even present in her own body.

As if in a trance, she moved down the hallway toward a room where Nader was seated at his desk. Behind him on the wall was a diagram of a woman's body, her bright pink nipples and genitalia depicted in lurid detail. She wanted to ask him how he had the courage to hang this picture on the wall, but she suddenly remembered the gravity of her situation and realized that the question was meaningless. The good doctor rose from his seat, took her hands in his, and kissed her on both cheeks.

"*Na-tarss, Shireen-joon*," he said, his voice neutral and serene. "You don't need to be afraid. It will be over quickly. But I must let you know that my associate, Dr. Mohit, will be performing the procedure for you. I'm sure you understand that being your relative, I cannot perform it myself."

She asked for and was given total anesthesia. When she woke up, Nader was sitting beside her bed.

"*Tamam shod*," he said. "It is over. I will drive you home now."

Shireen felt no physical pain at any time during the procedure or during the process of recovery. But she could not escape the sensation that the blood that seeped from her body was not her own, but Ahmad's.

A few weeks later, Shireen's parents announced that they would be sending her to California where she would live with her uncle and attend UC Santa Cruz. They had already secured a visa, and thanks to her uncle's connections her admission to the university was all but guaranteed. If her parents had learned of her affair, they didn't let on.

On the airplane that carried her away from Iran and toward her new life, she clutched the ram's horn in her hand and read *Another Birth*. Throughout her four years of college, she did her best to adapt to life in America. She became something of a chameleon, putting on different masks for different situations, but always feeling like an out-sider beneath them. She never wondered what the long-term effects of the cocaine and marijuana she consumed might be, never paused to consider the 180-degree turn she had taken. She graduated with a degree in anthropology, marched in her graduation ceremony, took the obligatory photographs of herself in cap and gown and mailed them to her parents in Iran. Often during those four years she felt as if these actions were being taken by someone else, and that she was just an onlooker.

During the summer vacation after her sophomore year, when she was visiting Tehran, Shireen called Ahmad's number. She sensed the truth even before it was pronounced by the quivering voice that came through the earphone: "Ahmad is in Evin Prison."

For years afterwards, she tried not to imagine the squalor she knew existed inside his prison cell: the rats that scurried through the pipes and across the floor; the cot soaked in blood and sweat; the cold cement floor; the buckets that held the shared waste of so many. She tried not to imagine torture. Execution. She did her best to picture him sitting, standing, walking, reading—whole and alive.

ꙮ

The sky had already darkened when Shireen returned from school that evening. Her mind had been full of Ahmad since she had read his email that morning, and she went about her household duties in a daze. Before getting into bed, she drank almost a full bottle of wine, but she was still too agitated to sleep. She couldn't arrest the visions that came pouring forth. Ahmad's benevolent face. His hands, slender but firm. His long, nimble body. Her mind spun forward and pictured him as he would be now, at age sixty-one. She pictured the child they might have had, who would now be thirty-four.

She got out of bed and went into the study, where she reached inside the desk drawer and picked up the ram's horn she had been carting around for more than three decades. She lifted it to her lips and blew it softly.

In the bedroom at the end of the hall, her husband's snoring continued unabated. He would not wake the rest of the night. The other bedrooms of the house were empty. Her two children were living their own lives now—they had long since broken the reins with which she once bound her life to theirs in willful self-exploitation. She no longer needed to turn her attention toward them constantly, like some paranoid backseat driver. She could do whatever she wanted.

She would later think of it not as a whim, but as a temporary suspension of free will that made her grab her purse, take out her wallet, and extract the scrap of paper with Ahmad's email address on it. Her body moved as if in a dream toward the computer, where the screen sat in blank anticipation, everything that came later already nascent, already predestined.

AAB

MINOO HASN'T BEEN INSIDE MANY HOTELS IN HER LIFE, so she isn't sure what to expect from the Azadi Hotel. While her parents are checking in, she assesses the cavernous lobby. Its walls are covered in gold wallpaper with a floral print that clashes badly with the blue and white carpet. There are clusters of uncomfortable-looking chairs here and there, all of which have a view of the three huge screens that are blaring the government television station. She looks up at the vaulted ceilings and notices that the chandeliers dangling from them are covered in a thick layer of dust. She knows the hotel was built before the Revolution, and she wonders if the chandeliers have been cleaned since then.

She glances over toward the reception desk, where her father is paying for the room. Her mother is standing behind him looking a bit awkward, as if she isn't certain what she is supposed to do in a hotel lobby or whether she should be here at all. Seeing her parents in these surroundings makes Minoo feel a rush of tenderness for them. It was a stretch for them to afford this trip, the first the family has taken in several years, and she knows they are doing it for her. The man behind the reception desk accepts the payment, then gives her father an envelope with the keys inside and points down the hallway toward the elevator.

The décor in the bedroom is tawdry, but it is clean. There is a king-size bed along one wall, covered in a bright bedspread topped with gleaming white pillows. Behind it, Minoo spots an alcove that holds a tidy single bed where she guesses she will sleep. There is only one window in the room, and its view is of an opulent but grimy building that Minoo's father told her used to be a gambling casino but is now a school. At the back of the room, a sliding glass door leads out to a balcony overlooking the Caspian Sea.

The six-hour drive along winding roads in her father's cramped Citroen had not been easy on Minoo's stomach, and after helping her parents unpack, she goes out onto the hotel balcony to watch the sun making its descent over the horizon. From up here on the fourth floor, the water looks blue and serene. The truth, Minoo knows, is quite another thing. It is common knowledge now that the Caspian Sea has become dangerously toxic. Oil refineries, industrial waste, radioactive waste, and untreated human waste have all been dumped into the sea for decades. Minoo has heard that the water has a foul odor and that suspicious-looking bubbles can be seen on its surface. But right now, from up here, she finds the seascape beautiful.

This is not Minoo's first visit to the Caspian seashore. She has been here one other time, when she was a child of nine or ten. During that trip, she had gone with her mother to the women's part of the beach, and they had gotten into the sea together. The women's beach was marked off from the rest of shoreline by a tall metal fence draped in black mesh that extended into the water and was closed off at the end. This hid the women from view and prevented them from venturing out far enough to mingle with the men, who were swimming freely on either side of the enclosure. Even though the men could not see them, Minoo and her mother were required to swim in their full hijab, including pants, a roopoosh, and a headscarf. Despite the discomfort, Minoo remembers the day as exhilarating. She and her mother frolicked together in the waves, made jokes about their wet hijab being revealing, and returned to the hotel room with their clothing drenched and covered in sand. She has not been in a body of water larger than a bathtub since that day.

Minoo and her parents do not intend to swim during this trip. They have come to the Caspian to get away from the noise and pollution of Tehran, to be together, and to relax. They plan to spend their days on the coast doing things they rarely have time to do: shopping together in the open markets, going to restaurants, and sightseeing in some of the small seaside towns. They will certainly stroll along the beach, perhaps gather some seashells and dip their toes in the water, but they have no intention of getting in. It's not just the toxicity; it's the fact that the beaches—those designated for men as well as those marked off for women—are now patrolled by angry female lifeguards covered from head to toe in black hijabs. They do not relish the thought of being scrutinized and screeched at by such women.

Even though she hasn't been in many bodies of water, water has always called to Minoo. The first word she learned to write as a child was *aab*—water. It is the word every child learning to read and write Farsi begins with, because it is made up of the first two letters of the alphabet: *aleph* and *be*. But to Minoo, learning to write this word had a special kind of significance. She remembers feeling entranced by the way the two letters on the page seemed to suggest the shape of a body of water with a tree beside it. She has always loved the sound of the word, the way it can be rolled around in the mouth and held in the throat for a long time. She loves looking at pictures of the world's beaches on the Internet and imagining herself there, standing on the shoreline. Whenever YouTube can be accessed, she watches videos of female swimmers. She is fascinated by their lithe, muscular bodies cutting gracefully through the water. At times, she almost feels she is inhabiting those bodies, inhaling and exhaling with the swimmers, gliding through the water herself.

∽

Minoo has often wondered whether her fascination with water might come from something she carries in her genes. On the wall in the apartment where she lives with her parents in central Tehran hang two photographs of her grandmother, Nasrin Hashemi. As a child, Minoo would stare at these photographs in awe and disbelief, trying to reconcile those images of her grandmother with the puffy-eyed, careworn woman she knows as Mamani. Whenever Mamani comes to visit them, she sits on the balcony smoking cigarettes and drinking endless cups of tea. How could Nasrin, the woman in the photographs, possibly be Mamani?

The photographs are grainy enlargements that have yellowed slightly with age, but what they depict is unmistakable. One of them shows a young Nasrin, probably seventeen or eighteen, huddled together with four other women who are around the same age. All of them are wearing green and white one-piece swimsuits and white swimming caps, and all of them are glistening with water droplets, obviously having just emerged from a pool. The other photograph is of Nasrin standing alone, her hands on her slender hips, wearing a tight floral one-piece swimsuit. In this photograph she has no swim cap, and her long, dark tresses spill around her shoulders. Both photographs are captioned: Iranian National Women's Swim Team, Asian Games, 1974.

When she grew older, Minoo learned to read the captions and place the photographs on the timeline of Iran's history. By then, of course, her mother had explained to her that Mamani had been a champion swimmer in the years before the Revolution. Women were still allowed to swim in 1974, and they were even allowed to wear bathing suits just as women did elsewhere in the world. It was not considered sinful at the time for women athletes to display their bodies in front of men. Men didn't just watch female swimmers— they followed them, supported them, cheered them on, and coached them.

Even now, at age sixteen, this seems unfathomable to Minoo. She knows, of course, that everything was different before the Revolution, that women wore miniskirts, went to nightclubs, danced and sang in public. In her classes at school, she has learned that these behaviors were part of Iran's "Westoxication"—its exposure to the decadence and corruption of Western countries, primarily the United States. What she has difficulty fathoming is that her grandmother had once been so physically fit, so thin and muscular, so full of energy and vigor. Throughout Minoo's life, Mamani has always been wrapped in dark, loose-fitting clothing that hides the shape of her rotund body. In the photograph, Nasrin is proudly parading her body. If one looks closely, the contours of her breasts are visible in the picture, and there is even a suggestion of her nipples. Perhaps the most shocking thing of all is the brazen way Nasrin is looking at the camera, as if to challenge the photographer, who must surely have been a man. The Mamani that Minoo knows often casts her eyes downward.

Just five years after these photographs were taken, when Nasrin was still in her heyday as a swimmer, Khomeini came to power. Almost overnight, women were forbidden to swim. Minoo's mother has told her that when she was growing up, Mamani rarely mentioned her swimming career. The pictures were not displayed in their home, and it wasn't until she was older that Minoo's mother learned her mother had been a competitive swimmer. When she discovered this, she asked Mamani if she could take swimming lessons, which were allowed in some of the female-only gyms in Tehran. Mamani just laughed at her and said, "In a hijab? That's not swimming, my dear daughter."

Whenever Mamani visits the apartment, she averts her eyes when she passes the photographs of herself. Minoo has never heard her comment on them at all, except to mutter something like "*Yaad-e-oon-roozha bekheyr.*" Those were the good old days. Although she won't say so directly, Minoo knows that it pains her grandmother to remember her years as a young woman who was free, not only to swim, but to go to discotheques and dance and laugh in the company of men.

Although she never talks about her years as a swimmer, Mamani follows the news about women's sports in Iran with great interest. A few years ago, she was outraged when she heard a story on the news about a female swimmer who swam for eight hours along the Caspian seacoast, breaking a record. She broke the record while wearing six kilos of clothing, including a full wet suit, a swimming cap, a scarf, and a cape covering her whole body. Her swim took place in a secluded part of the Caspian where there were no men present. And still, the authorities refused to register her time because her attire did not conform to Islamic norms.

More recently, Mamani was visiting when another heartbreaking news story came on television: a woman who was jailed for dressing like a boy and attending a men's soccer match set herself on fire in protest of her sentence, dying from the burns a few days later. Mamani burst into tears, cursed at the television, and ran from the room. When she came out later to have her tea, her eyes were even puffier than usual, and her hands shook as she lit her cigarette. She took a deep drag, and as she exhaled, she mumbled, "Those bastards!" through a cloud of smoke.

Mamani had an even stronger reaction when she heard a Grand Ayatollah and Islamic scholar addressing the topic of female athletes during a television interview. The moment has lodged in Minoo's memory because it was when she realized for the first time how much anger her grandmother was carrying around. The Ayatollah insisted that women should not participate in sports such as weightlifting because it ruined their bodies and compromised their femininity. Minoo remembers his exact words. "A woman who lifts weights is no woman," he said. "The integrity of a woman is defined by becoming a mother and nurturing her children."

As she watched the interview, Mamani shook her head in disgust. "*Madar-ghahbeh*! Motherfucker!" she shouted at the television screen. Minoo, who had never heard her grandmother use such shocking language before, turned and stared at her. Mamani made no apologies. She did not turn her eyes from the screen, but instead continued shouting at it. "You filthy dog! You call yourself a scholar? You call yourself a leader? Who are *you* to say what a woman should do with her body? Who are *you* to decide what is feminine and what is not?"

Some of the news about Iranian women athletes fills Mamani with glee. Whenever she hears about a female athlete defecting to another country, as many have done in recent years, she applauds them. "*Aafarin! Barak'Allah!*" she will say. "Good for you!" When she heard that a female alpine skier had been chosen to carry the flag at the Winter Olympics, she waved her arms through the air joyfully. "Hurrah! It's about time we joined the rest of the human race!"

Minoo's parents invited Mamani to accompany them to the seaside for this trip, but she declined. Minoo cannot help but think that the sight of water fills her grandmother with sorrow and longing. It is less painful for her to stay at home drinking tea and smoking cigarettes.

ॐ

On the last night they are in the hotel, Minoo and her parents turn in early so they can be rested for the long trip back to Tehran. Lying in her single bed in the alcove, Minoo cannot sleep. She does not toss and turn, but instead lies perfectly still for a long time, listening to the sound of the lapping waves mingled with the sound of her parents' gentle snoring.

She does not know what compels her to get out of bed. It is not a rational or deliberate decision. Soundlessly, she pulls back the covers, swings her legs over the mattress, finds her slippers with her feet, and slips them on. Using the light of the moon to guide her, she walks over to the place where her roopoosh and headscarf are hanging, lifts them from the hook, and puts them on over her pajamas. She opens the door gently, walks down the narrow hallway to the elevator and pushes the button for the lobby.

When she enters the lobby and sees a man behind the desk, she has a moment of panic, thinking she might be stopped and interrogated. She doesn't believe it is against the hotel's rules for a guest— even a young, unaccompanied woman—to leave the hotel room and go for a walk, but just in case, she quickly plans what she will say: she has a headache and needs to get some air. Men do not question women who say they are in any kind of pain, as this could be an indirect reference to their menstrual cycles. The man behind the desk looks up and sees her, but he makes no attempt to stop her.

Outside, the moon, which is almost full, shimmers on the surface of the sea. The air is brisk for May, and there is a gentle breeze. Minoo's roopoosh and headscarf flap around her as she walks, but the sensation is pleasant. The moon's reflection draws her forward, and she aims directly for it, then realizes that the light is everywhere at once, dancing all across the water. She sees no toxic bubbles and smells no foul odors.

Guided by the moon's light, she moves down the shoreline until she comes to the men's section of the beach, which is not enclosed by a fence. The hotel is some distance away, and there is no one else about. As soon as she realizes she is alone, she knows exactly what she wants to do, and she does not hesitate: she strips off her headscarf, her slippers, her roopoosh, and her pajamas, and deposits them on the shore. Then she walks, naked, into the water.

The water encircles her, caressing first her ankles, then her knees, then her inner thighs, then her breasts, then her shoulders. Finally, she submerges her full head under the sea until she feels her hair floating on the surface. She has never learned to swim, but her arms know what to do. She moves them with the rhythm of the waves, buoying her body and propelling it forward. Every part of her body comes alive.

Unafraid, she plunges deep below the surface again and again, like a fish. Each time she rises for a breath, she whispers, *"Aab, aab."*

COMING OUT, GOING UNDER

I T WAS NOT UNTIL early adulthood that Leila paused to ask herself how and when her sexual awakening had occurred. By the time she asked the question and began to feel that an answer was coming into focus, she had realized it was futile to articulate the answer because the main person she wanted to present it to—her father—was not going to listen anyway. She continued to cobble together a theory about the origins of her sexual identity, but the theory changed so often that it seemed to have a life of its own, and Leila felt helpless to pin it down.

It was certainly not a sudden awakening; there was no epiphany that prompted or preceded it. Nor was it a gentle or linear process. All she knew with certainty was that at some point between her past as a stubborn child in Iran and her present as a mature woman living in the United States, she felt the first stirrings of desire for women. Sometime after those first stirrings, she began to accept the inexorable push of them. Once she was living in the United States, she gradually began to accept the fact that she could not change her sexual orientation and that she would eventually have to construct a persona that used gay pride as a chief building material.

But this proved to be a challenge. Whenever her father came into the picture—when he was carnally present, when she spoke to him

on the phone, and even when she thought about him—the whole
structure began to feel fragile and shaky. She could never allow it to
crumble altogether, as this would cause her to crumble too. But it
shook often, and this was a painful way to live.

When she first met Maribel during her second year at Bryn
Mawr, Leila was so instantly smitten that she felt strong enough to
take on not only her father, but all of Iran, with its ridiculously anti-
quated notions about homosexuality and sexuality in general. Every
square centimeter of Leila's conscious mind was opposed to this di-
mension of her culture, but her emotional self could not respond to
things in such absolute terms. She wanted to believe that her Iranian
cousins would love her just the same if they knew the truth about
her; that they would look past the minor detail of her sexual prefer-
ence and remember that she was still their intelligent, strong-willed
Leila, the wild and clever cousin to whose creative genius they had
always deferred in their childhood games. Surely they could understand that the qualities they had seen in her then would still be alive
in the mature lesbian version of her.

In the crevices of her grown-up mind, though, she knew her
Iranian family members would never be able to separate the essential
Leila from the Leila they now envisioned sharing a bed with a woman. If they would allow themselves to get to know Maribel, Leila was
certain they would admire her intellect and find her rich life experience fascinating. But they would never get to know her because they
would brand her from the outset as a sexual deviant.

Maribel Garrido Martin was everything Leila wanted in a companion. In addition to being the smartest woman—perhaps the
smartest *person*—Leila had ever met, she was also a perfect physical
match, complementing Leila's physique in a yin-yang sort of way.
When they nestled together in bed, they fit together like a ball and
socket. Maribel's frame was angular, whereas Leila was compact and

curvy, with a thin waist and wide hips she had inherited from her paternal grandmother. Maribel told her that in certain positions she looked like a crouching cat, and jokingly referred to her hips as "haunches." In contrast to Maribel's hair, which was dark and lustrous and cascaded down her back, Leila wore her hair closely cropped, the cowlick she had possessed as a child always emerging despite her best efforts to tame it. Maribel had a long face that reminded Leila of a Botticelli painting, but Leila had the heart-shaped face and arched eyebrows of the women in Persian miniatures.

A fellow comparative literature major, Maribel had been sent abroad from her native Santander to study at Bryn Mawr. They met at a lecture titled "Women Artists as Activists: The Failure of Assimilation," given by world-renowned anthropologist Dr. Marion Chabot as part of the Alice Paul Lecture Series. At the champagne reception following the lecture, Leila, who was starry-eyed at the thought of being in the same room with Dr. Chabot, was impressed to see how blasé Maribel was about her proximity to such a towering figure.

During their brief conversation, each scanned the other's face for a sign. Although Leila felt awkward at the beginning of the conversation, she soon found herself at ease with the beautiful stranger. She even joked with Maribel about her initials, "MGM," and asked her if she was in any way connected to the media empire. Although no phone numbers were exchanged that night, a seed was planted, and both women went away feeling confident that something would soon sprout.

એ⁓

Two days later, Maribel appeared in the dining hall of Leila's dorm and plopped her tray down next to Leila's. It was a mere coincidence that Leila was doing research for a paper she was writing on the picaresque tradition in literature and was at that moment poring over dense passages of the Spanish classic *Lazarillo de Tormes*. Maribel met Leila's eyes as she looked up from the book.

"I can help you with that if you want. I had to almost memorize that book when I was in high school in Spain. Our high schools are more serious than yours, you know?"

Her accent, incongruous against the background noise of clattering dishes and silverware, made Leila's heart skip a beat. She trilled her r's, lengthened her *i* in the word "if" so it sounded more like *eef*, and pronounced high school *"high e-skool"*.

"Okay. Let me test you. Who is speaking here?" Leila read a passage of the text aloud to Maribel, taking care to pronounce the Spanish "c" and "z" with the proper Castilian lisp.

"Your Spanish is decent, but you have a *yanqui* accent," Maribel said, ignoring the challenge.

"I'm not sure what kind of accent you have, but it's beautiful."

"Let's take a walk, and I'll tell you all about Lazarillo. He is one of the greatest characters in all of Spanish literature. He is the quintessential Spaniard."

The walk led to dinner at a Mediterranean café and ended in Maribel's single dorm room. It was a given that they would spend every night together from that point on. During the day they met between classes, took long bike rides in the parks surrounding campus, attended plays and concerts and panel discussions and exhibits, read and studied together. They planned weekend getaways in Maribel's Honda Civic: to Pittsburgh and New York City and Chicago, to a cottage in the Poconos, to Niagara Falls, which Maribel had been determined to see since she first arrived in the United States. The relationship was so intense that both shut off their separate circles of friends, corresponded less frequently with their family members, and turned their attention almost exclusively to one another.

Despite her determination to build her life around Maribel, Leila was always frightened that someone would spot the two of them on campus together and be horrified to learn the truth. Maribel, on the other hand, was absolutely brazen in her public displays of affection—even sexual desire. She insisted on flaunting their relationship and derived a special thrill from walking with her arm around Leila in places she knew were frequented by men: baseball games, parks full of male joggers, local pick-up bars. There were many establishments in town that openly catered to gay patrons, but Maribel seemed to enjoy mixed company more. She insisted she didn't hate men, but she never missed the opportunity to define herself as their diametrical opposite. Maribel didn't just announce her lesbianism to everyone she met—she wore it like a badge.

One morning, during the breathless period that followed their lovemaking, they decided to skip their classes and remain in bed. Propping herself up on one elbow and stroking Leila's naked flank with her free hand, Maribel began to recount the story of her coming out. Leila's back was turned, but she could hear the levity in her lover's tone, the complete absence of guilt or shame.

"I was only fourteen at the time, but I already knew. I think my parents knew too, which was why they kept making such pathetic attempts to get me interested in boys. One day when my mother was going on and on about the handsome son of one of her friends, I just looked her in the eye and told her, *No me gustan los chicos, Mamá. Me gustan las chicas.* And that was it. I had come out."

Leila was familiar with the expression, but she had never known anyone, male or female, who had performed the action of "coming out." She turned over in bed and faced Maribel. "Just like that?"

"What do you mean 'just like that'? What did you expect me to do, bring in an orchestra and make a big production of it?"

"How did your parents take it?"

"They hated it. They hated me for a while too. I guess they don't hate me anymore, but I think they do prefer to have me safely on the other side of the Atlantic."

The idea of coming out to her college friends was frightening enough to Leila, but the idea of coming out to her parents was simply unthinkable. She knew her mother's love for her would not waver, but she couldn't bear to imagine the pain the news would cause her. The thought of coming out to her father was far, far worse. The blow would be so devastating that it would change him forever. More importantly, it would permanently destroy her relationship with him, which she already felt was threadbare. It would obliterate the last remaining shreds of love he felt for her. She would rather die than tell him.

She turned her face away from Maribel and buried it in the pillow. "I don't think I'm ready for that," she said.

Maribel did not hide her disappointment. "Are you telling me that the woman I have chosen as my partner is so cowardly and juvenile? You are almost twenty-three, Leila. Aren't you ready to form your own identity?"

When Leila tried to explain that Iranian culture judged homosexuality more harshly than it judged robbery, murder, or child abuse, Maribel laughed out loud. *"Por favor, hija mia!* Just because they *do* judge it that way doesn't make it *right* for them to judge it that way. You've taken sociology and anthropology classes, so you should know that not everything in a culture is sacred, no matter how old or traditional it is. Also, a culture is not unchangeable, you know. Do you have any idea how much Spain has changed in the years since Franco died? They didn't even have toilets for women in the bars during the Franco era because it was considered improper for women to drink in public. Today the bars are full of women."

"Yes, Maribel, but that's Europe. We're talking about Iran here. And we're talking about Islam. We're talking about the Islamic Republic. Any time religion comes into the picture, the rules become really convoluted."

"Remember that we have religion in Spain, too. Did you ever hear of Catholicism?"

❦

When Maribel invited Leila to accompany her to Santander that summer, her need to be honest with her parents came to a sudden head. They were expecting her to spend the summer in Iran as she always did, and her father had secured a few weeks of vacation time to accompany his family to their villa on the Caspian seacoast. Leila loved the Caspian, but how could she reject a once-in-a-lifetime offer to visit the coast of Cantabria, which was reputed to be one of the most beautiful spots in the world? And how could she turn down the prospect of six straight weeks of leisure time in the company of Maribel?

She toyed with the idea of lying to her parents and telling them the trip to Spain was part of her program of study. This would have been believable, since they knew she had an interest in Spanish litera-ture and had taken several courses in it. But she told herself that lying to them was not only immoral, but also impractical. Sooner or later, she would have to face the fact that she had two choices: either come out to her parents or lie to them forever. They would eventually have to accept the truth about her. It might as well be now.

A phone call would be the most practical method for delivering the shattering news, but Leila couldn't bring herself to pick up the phone and do it. She knew that the moment she heard her father's voice, full of love for her and anticipation about her upcoming visit, she would crumble. What she wanted to communicate would come out all wrong. She would couch the truth in deceptive rhetoric and might end up not presenting it at all. Or she would blurt it out in such harsh and absolute terms that she would hurt her parents even more deeply.

She would write them an email. Her parents' Internet service was spotty, and it often took them a long time to respond to emails. The wait would be agonizing. Nevertheless, it was the wisest choice.

Once she had made the decision to write rather than calling, Leila endured several days of utter torment. She woke herself up in the middle of the night to compose sentences in her head, found her mind drifting during class, and became unusually distracted and clumsy. Maribel was decidedly unhelpful during this waiting period. "Just write the damn letter and stop thinking about it so much!" became her refrain—and tired of hearing it repeated so incessantly, Leila began avoiding her.

After several fits and starts and lengthy drafts of dense, emotional prose that she discarded, Leila finally decided that a blunt and concise message would be best. A quick, surgical move, like extracting a tooth, would be easier for her to write and easier for her parents to handle. The pain would be acute, but it wouldn't last as long as it might if she wrote a rambling emotional piece that her parents would want to return to again and again. She ended up with a single straightforward page. She didn't mention her sexual orientation directly, but the letter made it clear:

My dear parents,

I will start this letter by asking you to take several deep breaths, as what you are about to read is going to hurt you. I would do anything in the world to avoid hurting you, but I have come to the realization that sooner or later, I must present to you a truth about myself that will inevitably hurt you no matter when I present it. I must ask you to try to pause and consider that the truth I am about to reveal about myself is not in my control, even though I know that this will not ease your pain.

I have met a woman here at Bryn Mawr, and she has changed my life. I will not deliver a long description of her or of our relationship in this letter. All I will say is that I love her in a way that I have never loved anyone in my life, and that she has helped me to realize who I am.

This woman, whose name is Maribel Garrido Martin, has asked me to spend the summer with her and her family in Santander, Spain. This is an opportunity I cannot turn down. I will have the privilege of visiting a beautiful country with a rich and fascinating history. More importantly, I will have the opportunity to become acquainted with the family and culture of the woman I love.

I am relieved to have said this to you, even though I know that I have left you feeling bewildered and heartbroken. I will always love you with all my heart, and I hope you will continue to love me too. Please call me when you receive this letter.

> *Your loving daughter,*
> *Leila*

No answer came for the next few days, and while she waited Leila found herself craving Maribel's company again, more than ever. She needed Maribel's constant chatter, her running commentary on the world around her, her incisive analyses of everything she saw and heard. She needed Maribel's strong, protective embrace in bed each night. She needed to feel that Maribel would somehow replace the parents she had alienated and possibly lost—that she would become mother, father, and lover all rolled into one. She needed to feel that Maribel was vital enough to make up for a whole country, a whole culture, and a whole history she had willfully given up.

⁓

By the time Mr. Farhani made the phone call to his daughter, he already had an elaborate plan in place and had created a network on the ground in the United States to help him execute it: an Iranian psychiatrist who had a private clinic in New York City, a brother-in-law Leila had always liked, and a travel agent. The psychiatrist would convince Leila that her condition was temporary and treatable. The brother-in-law would remind her of her Iranian heritage and would try to bring her back into the family fold. The travel agent would book two hotel rooms in Philadelphia, two plane tickets from Philadelphia to New York City, and two plane tickets from New York to Tehran.

The phone call was brief and businesslike. Mr. Farhani knew exactly what he wanted to say, and he said it so rapidly that Leila barely had a chance to speak at all. *"Salaam,* Leila-joon," he began, using the brightest and most affectionate tone he could muster. "It's your baba. I have read your letter, and I just wanted to let you know that I am flying to the United States on Tuesday so we can talk about this in person. I want to spend three days with you in Pennsylvania, and after that I want to take you to New York for the weekend. Is that okay with you?"

Leila's hands were trembling on the phone receiver, but she was comforted by her father's jovial, almost loving tone. "I guess so," she muttered.

When Maribel asked her about the phone call, Leila was not entirely truthful. "He's coming here for a few days," she said. "I hope you'll have a chance to meet him," she added, although she knew her father had no intention of laying eyes on Maribel.

He arrived in Philadelphia on schedule, and Leila met him at the airport. Instead of returning with her to campus, he took her out to dinner in Philadelphia and convinced her to stay in the hotel room he had already booked for her that night. He was soft and lighthearted over dinner, and the conversation was mostly comfortable. Fearful of souring the mood, Leila did not bring up Maribel at all, but toward the end of the meal, over a glass of brandy, her father broached the subject himself. He had carefully planned not only the content, but also the timing, of what he was going to say.

"Leila-joon, you are young," he began. "You cannot know what your true feelings are right now, and you certainly can't know what love is. This relationship that you think is so important is only one of many you will have in your life. You are just trying on a new identity that you have picked up at Bryn Mawr."

Leila wanted to interject that her feelings for Maribel had nothing to do with any of that, that they were deep and true. But her father spoke again before she had a chance to formulate her sentence.

"That school is not enough for you, azizam. It is too small, and it doesn't have enough to offer a woman of your intellect and ambition. It was a mistake for you to choose it in the first place. But it isn't too late to correct that mistake."

Leila was stunned. "Are you saying I should drop out? I have already started this semester, Baba-joon. I can't leave now."

"Your credits can be transferred very easily to another school, azizam. Perhaps a school like Duke University, for example? It has a better reputation than Bryn Mawr anyway, and I have many contacts there."

"But what about the friends I have made?"

"You can make new ones, can't you? There are all kinds of people at Duke, from all over the world. Men *and* women."

"What about—"

Mr. Farhani did not want to hear the name Maribel cross his daughter's lips. "Do you mean your trip to Santander? I will buy you a ticket. In fact, if you'd like, your mother and I would be delighted to accompany you there ourselves."

Leila looked into her father's face and saw that his expression was full of warmth and understanding. He placed his hand over hers on the table and squeezed.

"How would you like to travel with me to New York City tomorrow? We can stay for a few days with Amoo-Abbas and see all the museums, Broadway plays, and lectures you want to see. And you can have time to think about this."

Leila closed her eyes and nodded. A tear traveled down her face and plopped onto the edge of her plate. "I will need to get some things from my dorm, Baba-joon."

"I don't think you'll have time, azizam. It is late now, and the plane leaves early tomorrow morning. Let's just go back to the hotel and sleep. I will buy you whatever you need in New York."

Never one for theatrical displays of emotion, Leila wiped away her tears and recovered her composure. "Let's go, Baba-joon. I'm ready."

The visit with the psychiatrist the next morning in New York was brief. His approach was to present homosexuality as an aberration that resulted from a combination of genetic, hormonal, emotional, and environmental factors—a phenomenon that was completely reversible. Leila came out of the appointment with her head spinning, but when her father beamed at her from the waiting room, she smiled back.

As promised, Mr. Farhani treated his daughter like a princess over the next few days, taking her to high-end restaurants and on shopping sprees, going with her to visit gallery exhibits he had no interest in and plays whose messages escaped him completely. Amoo-Abbas was just as she remembered him, witty and affectionate. Leila was certain that Baba had told his brother about her relationship with Maribel, but Amoo-Abbas never once mentioned it. Instead, he reminisced with her about her childhood in Iran, told stories about her days as a wild and precocious child, and immersed her in memories of the beautiful country she had abandoned.

❧

Leila suspected her father had a plan in place, though she couldn't pinpoint the exact details. But she had a plan of her own: she would appease her father for now, take a semester off, travel back to Iran and spend the next few months deepening her relationship with him, then return to the United States in the fall and begin a secret life as a gay woman. Her love for Maribel was strong, but the promise of restoring her father's pride in her—of basking in his love—was stronger. If Maribel lacked the sensitivity to understand the importance of family ties in Iranian culture, and if she didn't care enough to wait for her, then maybe she wasn't worth it to begin with.

On the night before they boarded the plane for Iran, Mr. Farhani encouraged Leila to call Maribel. He didn't protest when she closed herself up in the bedroom in Amoo-Abbas's house to make the call. He could hear her sobbing from behind the door, and when she emerged, he embraced her and allowed her to continue sobbing on his shoulder.

For the remainder of that school year and the long, hot summer that followed it, Leila languished in her childhood home in northern Tehran. Her parents made attempts to entertain her, introducing her to men and women her age, hosting parties in her honor, taking her to the Caspian seashore, buying her clothing and books and imported foods. She preferred to stay indoors, as she did not feel comfortable with the mandatory hijab. Her parents had installed a large-screen television in her room, but Iranian programming was shameless propaganda and it was almost impossible to connect to any foreign streaming services, so she had no interest in turning it on.

She had left her laptop behind in the States, but Internet service was spotty and the government had blocked most of the sites she might have wanted to connect to anyway. It was easier, for now, to remain detached from the world outside her windows. She spent long hours lying on her bed reading, listening to music, and dreaming up plans for escape.

Mr. Farhani sensed that his daughter was sinking into depression. One afternoon, he knocked on the door of her bedroom and presented her with a shiny new MacBook Air. "This is the newest computer on the market, azizam. It has something called an M2 chip. I'm not sure what that is, but I'm told it makes the computer very efficient. I know the Internet is frustrating in Iran, but I thought you might want to do some writing."

Touched by the gesture, Leila rose from her bed and hugged her father. "Thank you, Baba-joon," she said. "I'm sure I will use it."

For the first few days, she didn't do much besides play around with its camera, its sound system, and its other impressive features. But during a family gathering one evening, a cousin who was studying computer engineering at the university approached her and handed her a piece of paper listing four VPNs she could use without being detected. "I didn't tell your father I was giving you these," he said, flashing her a mischievous smile. "At the bottom of the list, there's the URL of a network you might want to check out."

As soon as the last family member had left, she went straight into her bedroom, closed the door, pulled out her laptop, and added the Surfshark VPN. Within seconds, she was able to connect to 6Rang, the network whose URL her cousin had scrawled at the bottom of the paper. She was astonished to learn that it was an Iranian Lesbian and Transgender network, and even more astonished to discover it had been established in 1995 and had hundreds of LGBTI+ subscribers who lived in Iran.

There were links on the website to many recent articles about imprisonment, forced marriage, mandatory conversion therapy, and other acts of violence against Iranians like her, and Leila trembled as she scrolled through these. But when she read the network's history and vision, her heart swelled with hope. 6Rang's mission was to raise awareness about violations of the rights of queer Iranians, and to eradicate homophobia, transphobia, and violence against members of the Iranian LGBTI+ community. Among the many services the organization provided was online counseling for queer individuals.

In the About Us section, there was an angry rant about Iran's discriminatory laws that favored heterosexual males and about the patriarchal power structure that was so deeply rooted in Iranian culture. Leila couldn't help but think of Baba. Part of her wanted to march straight into his bedroom and read the statement to him—but a larger part felt sorry for him, because he was so hopelessly brainwashed and behind the times.

She closed the laptop and looked out her bedroom window. There was a patch of blue peeking through the putrid cloud that hung over the city, and she could hear the chirping of birds and crickets above the din of Tehran traffic. For the first time since she had been back in Iran, she felt a twinge of hope. The city seemed to be calling out to her, letting her know she was not alone.

She would never be able to change her father, but she suddenly felt no need to do so. All she needed to move forward was to remember who she was.

THE DAUGHTERS

THE DAUGHTERS FILLED OUT their paperwork, renewed their passports, reserved their tickets, packed their suitcases, and flew halfway around the world to their parents' apartment in northern Tehran.

They were tourists in their own country. The parents noticed this in every conversation the daughters held in stilted Farsi, in their new gestures that seemed copied from an American television program, in every request they made to be driven to the bazaar or the chelow-kababi as if these normal features of everyday life in their country had become exotic to them.

They marveled over fresh fruit from their grandfather's orchard, declaring it to be like no fruit they had ever tasted even though they had eaten fruit from these same trees throughout their childhoods.

They went on shopping expeditions and returned with mundane objects: souvenirs made for foreigners, clay vases and ordinary tea-pots and cheap factory-made tablecloths, packaging them with care and storing them lovingly in their suitcases as though they were precious treasures.

During the day they drove through the streets of Tehran, looking out the window at the neighborhood they had once lived in, at the corner baq'aali where they had once bought toys and candies and batteries, at the walls of the school they had once attended.

They were surprised by the open sewers that lined the sides of the streets in Tehran, the *jubes* they had stepped over casually every day of their young lives. They were repelled to notice now, as if for the first time, that debris floated in the jubes and that the water in them was fetid.

They sounded out the signs on the streets and in the shop windows and the slogans painted on the walls in an effort to prove, perhaps to themselves most of all, that they had not become illiterate in their native language.

One afternoon when they were in town, the daughters were accosted by the Gasht-e-Ershad, the Morality Police who trolled the streets of the city in olive-colored Range Rovers looking for violations of the dress code. The officer who stopped them was a woman in a heavy black chador. She was a khahar, one of the "sisters" who were proud members of the brigade.

The khahar approached the younger daughter first. She thrust a gloved hand out from beneath her chador and extended her pointer finger toward the three-inch triangle between the knot of the daughter's headscarf and the top button of her roopoosh, lightly touching the skin. "Sister, your chest is showing," she said.

Next the khahar turned her attention toward the older daughter. Again she used her fingers, this time thrusting them toward her face and laying them on the faint lipstick the older daughter was wearing. In a voice trembling with anger, she told her, "That lipstick is martyr's blood."

The younger sister tightened her headscarf and the older one lifted the back of her hand to her mouth and wiped her lips. They promised to be more respectful in the future, and the khahar let them go.

They told their mother about the incident as soon as they got home, erupting into giggles as they spoke. The mother had lived with the morality police for many years and had nothing but scorn for the group's backward notions of feminine propriety. Still, it disturbed her to see her daughters ridiculing something that had become a fact of life in their country, something she herself had to contend with daily. She imagined her daughters telling their friends in California about the incident, all of them reacting to it with smugness and derision and glee.

Each night during their three-week visit, the daughters sat with their parents in the living room and drank *araq*, the alcohol their father bought illegally from Armenian men who brought it to the back door late at night disguised in opaque containers. Their mother, who had never taken a drink of araq in her life and worried about her husband's intake of the vile substance, was shocked to see her daughters drinking. She was even more shocked when they declared araq to be the best drink they'd ever imbibed, even though it was distilled in filthy basements from unwashed raisins.

Their father was mostly a silent listener during their conversations, which were often about places or subjects he knew nothing of. Occasionally when his daughters reminisced about their childhood, he spoke up to adjust their memories. When the conversation turned to Iranian politics or history, his daughters looked at him with genuine interest and expectation on their faces. He supplied the information they asked for, information he sensed they wanted to store in their brains for later use. But even when they prodded him, he did not hold forth the way he had done when they were younger.

During the day they took photographs, pulling out their cell phones every few minutes and snapping pictures. What were they photographing, the parents wondered. They could find no pattern in the subject matter of the photographs, no rhyme nor reason as to what their daughters wanted to immortalize.

They photographed the traffic. They photographed the storefronts, the bakeries, the fruit stands with their pyramids of cherries and quince and pomegranates, the piles of *sabzi,* the butcher shops with flies resting on the sides of beef.

They photographed the murals on the walls: the bearded "heroes" of the Islamic Revolution looking stern and defiant; the martyrs' faces painted in surreal colors with their eyes looking heavenward; the lurid depictions of the carnage supposedly caused by "The Great Satan" called America and its evil minion, Israel.

They photographed the smog-stained sides of buildings and the road signs and the billboards. They photographed the carts that lined the streets, the cigarette vendors and watermelon vendors and the vendors of cheap plastic goods hawking their products in the scorching heat.

The photographs had been taken on their cell phones, but the daughters decided they wanted prints. When the photographs came back from the shop, the daughters sat in the living room with their parents and passed them around. For some reason the parents couldn't understand, the photographs made their daughters chuckle. One of the photographs they found especially humorous depicted the storefront window of a clothing shop.

When her turn came to look at this picture, the mother wondered at first what was so amusing about it. She examined it more closely and saw that behind the window hung T-shirts with lettering in crooked, ungrammatical English. On the front of one T-shirt was a cartoon of a small, rosy-cheeked child wearing a big pink hat. Beneath the cartoon were the words AMERICAN GIRL. Another T-shirt had the words I AM IRANIAN LOVE MACHINE scrawled in white cursive letters inside a bright red heart. Emblazoned across the front of another T-shirt was the single word UNIVERSITY.

More photos were passed around, and the merriment continued. But when one photograph reached the mother's hands, she stood up and left the room. It was a photograph of a handwritten sign tacked to a wooden telephone pole. The sign advertised a kidney for sale.

Three weeks later, the daughters packed their suitcases with their new treasures and secured their cameras in their purses and donned their Islamic clothing in preparation for their flight back to the United States. The flight was scheduled to depart at four a.m., which meant that they had to leave home at one. Afraid they would be late, the parents didn't even attempt to sleep. They were bleary-eyed during the drive to the airport, but their daughters were giddy, marveling at the volume of traffic in the city even at this ungodly hour, anticipating the moment when they finally boarded the plane and could free themselves of their hijabs, talking excitedly about what they would do as soon as they were "home."

The parents embraced them at the security checkpoint and told them in trembling voices to be safe and to call often. As soon as their daughters vanished from sight, both parents shed quiet tears.

Their tears dried as they made the long drive back from the airport. Exchanging only a few words with one another, they turned the key in the apartment door, removed their shoes and sank their feet into the carpet, plugged in the samovar and prepared their tea, then sat and looked out the window at the grey sky above Tehran that was now streaked with the first rays of morning light.

VENUS FURTIVA

THE ONLY PART OF Zohreh's being she had ever loved unconditionally was her body. She subjected it to scrutiny often, like she did the other dimensions of herself, and it alone passed muster. Whenever she studied herself in the full-length mirror on her closet door, she was filled with awe for the curves of her hips, the angles of her shoulder blades, the contours of her lean back and legs. Her body was her constant companion—as faithful as a dog, as warm and sensual as a cat, and less demanding than either.

Zohreh told herself that she was entitled to feel this tiny shred of self-love at age twenty-seven, when she was at the height of her physical beauty and power—but everywhere she turned, someone seemed to be giving her guilt for it. If she were Catholic, she might get by with an abject confession and a string of Hail Marys. If she were Baptist, it would be enough just to smile innocently at church every Sunday and say her prayers when others were looking.

Things were a little more complicated for a young woman born in Iran and raised in an affluent Iranian community in the heart of Buckhead. There was nowhere to confess and there were no pardons to be granted. She didn't know any prayers, and her innocent smiles didn't fool anyone. But whenever she tried to just be herself, it backfired. Silence would fall around her every time she entered a room full of Iranians. The women would bat their mascaraed eyelashes and give her huge lipsticked smiles, then lean together to whisper about her behind their hands as soon as she turned her back. It would almost be easier to live in Iran and face stoning. At least that would be a clear fate. She had never understood the logic by which it was morally acceptable to shame a woman, even stone her to death, for going against the alleged "will" of a made-up male deity, but morally unacceptable for a woman to love the body that same male deity supposedly endowed her with.

Like most Iranian mothers, Zohreh's mother had raised her to believe that her body should be kept in a cage—or better yet, on a pedestal. Maman regarded women's bodies the same way she regarded sculptures and paintings: they were decorative items intended for the pleasure of others, to look at but not to touch. She enjoyed dressing Zohreh and her sister Ladan in crisp, name-brand clothing, but she was uncomfortable with any direct mention of her daughters' bodies, or of the female body in general. When they were growing up, Zohreh and Ladan often found their minds flooded with questions about their emerging womanhood: menstruation, puberty, boys, sex. But they knew better than to ask their Maman to give them answers. Instead, they just whispered their own theories to one another, getting everything wrong.

The movie *Chicago* came out when Zohreh was in middle school, and she quickly became a devotee. She found the glorification of husband-killers amusing, and it gratified the part of her that harbored anger against the boys who taunted her at school. But the film touched a deeper, more buried part of her psyche, a part she couldn't pinpoint. She loved the costumes, the stockinged legs, the scarlet lipstick, the sultry voices, the suggestive scenes, and the lurid images that these things conjured up in her mind. She especially loved the dancing. She bought a DVD of the film with money she stole from her mother's purse and watched it again and again until she knew every beat of the songs by heart and could mimic all the dance moves. As she undulated her body to the smoky female voices, she fell almost into a trance. It was like being rocked in an embrace.

Chicago started her quest for other movies in the same vein, and she soon discovered *Cabaret*. She became so obsessed with this movie that at one point she convinced her mother to let her chop off her waist-length hair so she could look more like Liza Minnelli. Her arched eyebrows and high cheekbones bore no resemblance to Minnelli's vaguely rodent-like features, but she examined herself in the mirror, pursing her lips and tossing her head in a pathetic attempt to mimic her favorite heroine. She plunged deeper and deeper into the performance underworld until she reached a point where the seamier, the sleazier, the more degenerate the performance was, the more wholeheartedly she embraced it.

Her mother didn't know about any of this, of course.

ত৩

When she moved away to UGA and was finally free from the scrutiny of her mother, Zohreh was sucked into the sordid world of college sex. As soon as the men she slept with tried to stake a claim on her, though, she felt trapped. Determined to reclaim herself, she moved to Atlanta after graduation and rented a small studio in Cabbagetown. A few days later, she waltzed into a tiny, smoke-filled bar in Atlanta called Southern Exposure, auditioned, and was hired as a performer.

During the day she was Zohreh Hakim, a biostatistician with a respectable job and a decent income. But at night she became Venus, a provocative burlesque dancer. She chose the stage name because it was the literal translation of her Persian name, but also because she liked the connotations: goddess of love and desire; ideal of female beauty; born from the foam of the sea; venerated by men and women alike. It was a fitting name for her secret alter ego, her Ms. Hyde.

Shortly after Zohreh began dancing, her mother happened upon a Facebook post advertising an upcoming show at the club. A single click led directly to a photo of Zohreh stretched out on piece of satin, her cleavage accentuated by the camera angle, her lips slightly parted, her eyes glancing sleepily up at the camera from beneath heavily made-up lids. The caption read: "Come see VENUS, our dreamy new goddess, at Southern Exposure this Saturday night!"

When her horrified mother confronted her about the photo, Zohreh did some quick thinking. "It's just a joke, Maman-joon. Some of my old college friends thought it was funny to post that about me. I'm so busy at work right now that I barely have time to notice what's on my Facebook page."

"Okay, azizam," Maman said, her voice soft and maternal. "But please be more careful. And tell your friends that their jokes can get you in trouble."

Her mother's effortless acceptance of her flimsy explanation stunned Zohreh and filled her with tremendous guilt and sadness. She immediately took the photo down, and for several days afterwards she was unusually deferential around her mother, who quickly forgot about the incident. But even with the picture gone, Zohreh knew she wouldn't be able to hide her new passion from her sister. Ladan spent a great deal of time online and was a master at prying into other people's lives. She didn't really need hard evidence from photographs or Facebook posts; she had an uncanny ability to read her sister's mind and could interpret even the subtlest of behaviors with unerring precision. And so, wishing to preempt her sister's discovery, Zohreh confessed to her one afternoon when they were having coffee together at Starbucks.

Ladan reacted with a degree of disapproval bordering on disgust. "So, let me get this straight," she said. "You are willfully participating in your own objectification?"

Zohreh had not expected this kind of old-school, textbook feminism from her highly educated, supposedly progressive sister. She put down her coffee cup and stared at her in disbelief.

"Really, Ladan? You have a problem with women asserting their sexual power? This is the twenty-first century. Haven't you ever heard of neo-feminism?"

"Give me a break, Zohreh. I don't care what trendy terms you want to attach to it. It's basically just stripping."

"Oh, my God! I would never have imagined my own sister to be such a philistine! Burlesque is one of the few counter-narratives we have to the one that says women have to conform to beauty norms set by men. It's not about women pleasing men—it's about women pleasing themselves, being in touch with their own bodies. Why don't you try opening your mind a little?"

Ladan took a sip of her coffee, put the cup down loudly, and fixed Zohreh in a stare. "You can put all the bullshit intellectual spin on it you want to, *khahar-joonam*. As far as I'm concerned, it's one step away from porn."

Zohreh was becoming agitated, but she delivered her defense in as steady a voice as she could muster. "First of all, Ladan-joon, it might interest you to know that even porn is now considered a form of liberation by some neo-feminists. But burlesque is actually ANTI-porn. Think about it. It's women doing what they want rather than what men want. It's not exploitative or demeaning; it's empowering and uplifting. It's like a celebration of self."

"Wow. Listen to yourself, Zohreh. Where did you pick up all that jargon?"

Ladan was right: she did sound like she had just walked out of a women's studies class. But she believed what she was saying, and she was determined to press her point.

"You've been to college, right? Then you should know that burlesque has a long and reputable history. It's actually a form of performance art. It's satire. Haven't you seen *Cabaret*? That movie takes place in Nazi Germany, remember? Burlesque flourishes in repressed societies. It has a context. Not to mention the fact that burlesque troupes are connected to all kinds of progressive organizations. Even the tiny bar where I dance donates money to the AIDS foundation."

At this point Ladan was barely looking Zohreh in the eye, and she had a tremor in her voice. "I won't stop you from doing it, or even judge you for doing it. But please don't ask me to go see you perform, okay?"

No matter what her sister thought of her dancing, Zohreh wasn't about to give it up. She couldn't help herself—she simply loved it. She loved the women who performed it; the woman-heaviness of it. She had read about Venus cults where statues of the goddess were ceremonially removed from the temple by virgins, taken to underground baths, undressed, bathed, and garlanded in myrtle. Being a burlesque dancer was like being part of this powerful cult. She believed in it, and she needed it. She would just have to be more careful to keep her burlesque identity a secret from her mother, her father, her sister, and the entire Iranian community.

∾

One Saturday morning, as Zohreh drew the curtains aside to let in the early morning light, she had a vision for a stunning new burlesque number. It came to her when her eyes fell on an Iranian doll that sat on her bookshelf, pushing forward a memory that played in her mind with cinematic intensity.

It was summer, and Zohreh was in Iran with her mother to visit her grandparents. The day was sweltering, as summer days in Tehran often are, and Maman and her mother Madar-jaan wanted to take Zohreh and Ladan out for faloodeh, the cold rosewater and corn-starch confection both girls loved. Despite the heat, Maman and Madar-jaan had to dress in full hijab, but Zohreh and Ladan were still young enough to go out uncovered. The warm breeze caressed Zohreh's bare legs and blew through her long, dark hair as she walked down the sidewalk.

Just as they were nearing the faloodeh stand, Zohreh's eyes fell on a doll in the window of one of the general stores that lined the streets of Tehran. The display in the window was cluttered and dusty, but she could see the doll peeking out from behind the jumble of waste-baskets, tablecloths, notebooks, and other household items. She was made of cheap plastic and dressed in a glittery tribal costume of gar-ish mismatched fabrics. Her crude, painted-on features were frozen in an unnatural stare, more of a grimace than a smile.

When Zohreh asked her mother if she could have the doll, Maman instantly refused. "That is the ugliest doll I have ever seen, Zohreh! Why on earth would you want to have a doll like that when you can have all those beautiful dolls that they sell in the States?"

Ladan, a full year older and no longer prone to such childish desires, laughed at Zohreh for wanting such a foolish toy. "I thought you were too old to play with dolls," she said derisively.

But Zohreh looked at the doll and she knew with certainty that the doll was looking back at her, crying out to her. She begged her mother again, and this time, thanks to Madar-jaan's gentle prodding, she gave in.

Back at her grandparents' house, she lifted the doll from her box, held her at arm's length, and examined her. The more she stared at the doll's rigid expression, the more she felt her softening, coming alive. The doll seemed to be pleading with her for release. On a sud-den whim, Zohreh began to undress her.

She started with the outer skirt, which had an elasticized waist-band and came off easily. Then she proceeded to the trousers the doll was wearing beneath her skirt, which were loose fitting and also came off with no difficulty. Underneath these garments, the doll's plastic legs glistened on either side of a sexless trunk. It startled Zohreh to discover that her doll was not wearing underwear, and she resolved to get some for her as soon as she could.

Next she turned her attention to the upper part of the doll's body, which was clothed in a shiny red blouse with gold stripes streaking through it, and a short, loose vest of green fabric. She removed the vest with a single movement of her fingers. But the blouse resisted: it was glued to the plastic and couldn't be lifted from the doll's body. Frustrated, she began to yank at the cloth until it gave way with a sudden sibilant sound.

She was not prepared for what she found. The doll had no breasts, no semblance of a woman at all. Her chest had been painted green to look like an undergarment of some kind, and there was just a vague bulge where her breasts should have been. Zohreh hastily closed up the fragments of the blouse and put the vest back on. Then she touched the headscarf the doll was wearing and discovered that it, too, was glued on. Fearing that her hair might also be nothing more than paint, she made no attempt to remove the doll's headscarf. She did not want to face any more truths about her doll, so she put her back in her box. It was years before Zohreh removed her again.

Zohreh's sudden vision that Saturday morning filled her with a sense of purpose: her burlesque number would finally allow her, symboli-cally at least, to give the doll the freedom she deserved. When she stripped down to her own very real pudenda and breasts, the doll would finally possess these features, and they would spring to life before the audience.

From a trunk at the foot of her bed, Zohreh pulled out a tribal outfit she had bought on a trip to Iran a few years earlier—a gorgeous Qashqai costume with an intricately embroidered tunic, a billowing skirt, and a long flowing headscarf bordered in sequins. She slipped it on and looked at herself in the full-length mirror. The costume was a little tight, but she liked the contrast between the form-fitting tunic, which accentuated the contours of her breasts, and the full skirt and trousers, which gave a subtle hint of the shape of her hips and legs. She turned this way and that in the mirror, watching as the skirt swished around her calf muscles in a shimmering spiral.

She picked up the scarf and draped it around her body as she had learned to do in Iran, flinging the loose ends over her shoulders. This would make it easier to remove. She practiced draping it and removing it several times until she could do it gracefully. She practiced removing the skirt and the trousers. Both were elasticized as the doll's had been, and she had no difficulty getting them off with a few gentle movements of her fingers and a slight swiveling of her hips.

The top was going to be trickier. She didn't want to destroy her costume, but she could engineer the tunic with snaps going down the front so it could be removed wholesale with a single swift move. Beneath the costume she would wear sheer thigh-high stockings, a garter belt, and her favorite stilettos.

☙

It was about 9:30 when Zohreh arrived at Southern Exposure and pulled into the back parking lot. An eerie cloud of orange hung low over the bar, and above it the sky was roughly the color of cement. Even with her windows rolled up, she detected the putrid stench emanating from the dumpsters at the back of the club, and as soon as she entered the alleyway leading to the side door, it hit her full force.

Inside the air was already thick with cigarette smoke. Backlit by the neon lights of the bar, it curled up toward the ceiling, creating a visual effect Zohreh found mesmerizing, almost beautiful. She had never been a smoker herself, but something about tobacco appealed to her. It didn't connote ill health; it connoted conversation, passion, and warmth. Perhaps this was because her father, like many Iranian men of his generation, was a heavy smoker who scoffed at the health warnings and insisted on smoking in the house. Once when Zohreh was asked to draw a picture of her family in elementary school, she drew Baba with a cigarette in his hand and a cloud of smoke above his head. Her scandalized teacher called home, only to be told to mind her own business.

For some reason, Zohreh's thoughts often turned to her father whenever she was preparing to perform a burlesque number. She imagined the look that might cross his face as he watched his daughter removing her clothes on stage—a look that combined shame, embarrassment, and unqualified sorrow. Picturing her father in the lead-up to a performance usually had the effect of cold water on a fire, and she had to force herself to switch channels so she could get in the right mood for dancing. But tonight, she willfully conjured his face as she walked into the bar, holding it in her imagination for as long as she could. It hurt, but it felt strangely cathartic.

Zohreh had never been fond of the women's dressing room scene, mostly because the act of preparing for a number was intensely personal for her. Putting on her costume and doing her makeup was almost a mystical experience—a sort of sublimation and rebirth. She needed to go through the ritual alone, and she had completed most of it at home tonight. She went backstage only for long enough to say a quick hello, change into her stilettos, and hang up the raincoat she was wearing over her costume. There wasn't room to wait in the wings, so the dancers always sat at the tables lining the sides of the stage. She entered the club and seated herself in a dark corner where she couldn't be easily spotted.

One of the waiters at Southern Exposure, a young Pakistani named Nawaz, caught sight of her and came out from behind the bar with a glass in his hand. He approached Zohreh's table and set a whiskey ginger down in front of her.

"You okay?"

She didn't look up as he asked the question, but she thought she detected a touch of derision in his voice. Zohreh liked Nawaz, but something about him had always unnerved her. Being an employee of the club, he couldn't very well disapprove of burlesque dancing, but for some reason every time she danced in front of him, she felt his eyes boring through her, as though he were seeing not her nude body but her naked soul.

"Yeah, I'm fine. Just a little nervous about tonight's number."

"I'm sure it will be amazing, like always." He winked at Zohreh and touched her shoulder gently, then turned back toward the bar.

Sipping her whiskey ginger, she watched the acts that came before hers, feigning interest but feeling detachment. When Mandy came up on stage, she jolted to attention. Mandy, whose stage name was Mimi LaDouce, was a large-breasted blond of about thirty-five whose husband had left her the previous year, taking their two children with him. Zohreh admired the way Mandy danced, pouring every ounce of her boundless energy into her dancing, holding nothing back. Seconds after she began dancing, before she had removed so much as a glove, the audience began shouting.

"Yeah, baby! Take it off!" Mandy fed their excitement and they fed hers. By the time the name Venus was called, they were in a state of near frenzy, shouting out across the floor.

"Come on, sister!"

"Let's see what you've got!"

"We love you, Venus!"

Zohreh gulped down the last of her drink, stood up and made her way onto the stage, the whoops and roars swelling behind her. As soon as she stepped out of the darkness and into the orb of spotlight, the catcalls and wolf whistles stopped, and silence fell as sharply as a blow with a machete.

She was covered from head to toe in her Iranian tribal costume; only the tiny oval of her face showed. This was something that the audience at Southern Exposure had never seen before, and they weren't quite sure how to react. She couldn't see too well with the spotlight in her eyes, but she could sense squirming in the audience.

The first track she had put together for her number was classical Iranian music, deep and plaintive. She stood stock-still on stage for the first four measures, looking out ahead of her but avoiding eye contact with the audience. Then, as the music rose in pitch and volume, she began to move, at first only turning her head stiffly from side to side, and then gradually making mechanical, puppet-like movements as though she were being pulled on strings. When she had completed the awakening of her body, she moved downstage and began to remove her outer layer of clothing.

The next track on the compilation was Persian belly dance music, deeply percussive. She had never learned belly dancing, which was an art form, but she could mimic some of the undulations of the ribcage, hips, and arms. She started to undress, her movements matching the beat of the track. She began with the vest, removing it jerkily, still in puppet mode. Her movements became more fluid as she removed the trousers, lifting each leg and pointing each toe in turn. She took off the elasticized trousers slowly, swiveling her hips as she pulled them down inch by inch. Next, she turned her back to the audience and slid her skirt down to the floor, lifting the tunic slightly to expose the bottom rim of her garter. Still wearing the tunic, she turned back toward the audience, reached up, and removed the headscarf, passing it across her arms and stroking her face with it as she did so. After she tossed it aside, she unfastened her hair and shook it loose until it cascaded down her back.

Several minutes into her number, the audience, usually screaming wildly by this point in a dance, was still mute. They remained mute when she leapt down from the stage and began to weave through the tables, swiveling her hips at exactly eye level. She ended the number back on stage again, where she picked up her headscarf and wrapped it demurely around her body, then crumpled to the floor.

Even with her head buried in her arms, she could sense the audience reacting as though they were emerging from hypnosis, offering a bit of polite applause above the murmuring and whispering. She lifted herself from the floor, took a bow, and dashed off the stage. She couldn't bear the thought of returning to her table inside the club, of anyone buying her a drink and making patronizing, clueless comments about her number.

Avoiding eye contact with the audience, the bartenders, and her fellow dancers, she shot into the dressing room, grabbed her raincoat, and exited the club through the back door. It was past midnight, but the streets of downtown Atlanta were still lined with cars, their taillights winking on and off at each intersection.

Making her way north on the interstate, she thought back over tonight's performance and the reaction to it. How many members of that audience, she wondered, would use her number to reinforce their belief that it sucked to be a Muslim woman? She detested Islam's screwed up ideas of womanhood—but she detested this narrative even more. She wasn't sure exactly what she had been trying to say with her number, but whatever it was had failed to penetrate those thick skulls. Maybe Ladan was right after all. Maybe what she was doing was just glorified stripping.

As soon as she walked into her apartment, she headed straight for the bathroom. What was she looking for when she examined herself in the mirror? The face that looked back at her was not the face of a performance artist—it was the face of a clown. She grabbed the gold bar of Dial and worked it through her hands under the faucet until it formed a rich lather, then lifted it to her face and began to scrub. She had forgotten to remove the false eyelashes, and one of them fell into the sink, sticking to the side of the bowl. It looked like a dead spider.

She stripped free of her raincoat and discarded it on the bathroom floor, and when she looked back into the mirror, she realized that the pasties were still on. She yanked them off, painfully, and tossed them into the wastebasket. She usually slept in the nude, but tonight she grabbed a T-shirt from the hook on the inside of the bathroom door and pulled it over her head. She didn't love her own body right now. She didn't even want to remember it was there.

When she got in bed, she turned her face to the wall and hugged her quilt to her chest. Closing her eyes, she breathed in the odor of her own sweat-drenched body, mixed together with the vague rosewater aroma of Madar-jaan, who had made the quilt for Zohreh years ago from remnants of old clothing. She conjured the face of her dead grandmother now, and she suddenly remembered the family legend about how she had once removed her shoe in the middle of a street in Iran and used it to slap a mullah she thought was ogling her young daughter.

That daughter was Zohreh's mother, who was now blithely sleeping in her house in America and had no idea who her own daughter was.

MANY SIDES

I T WAS BEGINNING TO FEEL ALMOST LIKE A RITUAL, this predawn awakening and the pattern of behaviors that followed it. First, Azita's eyes would spring open as if a button had been pushed somewhere at the back of her neck. Then, while her vision was adjusting to the faint light seeping in through the bedroom window, she would release her arm from beneath the pillow she always cradled while she slept and reach toward the nightstand to pick up her cell phone. The time was almost always somewhere in the four o'clock hour. Often it was exactly 4:17 when she looked at her phone, and the eerie recurrence of this time gave her a sense of foreboding. She had tried her own version of numerology on the three digits, but she never came up with anything. Perhaps this was a message from a higher power she wasn't sure she believed in; maybe 4:17 was going to be the hour of her death.

She would lie in bed for a few minutes waiting for her brain to boot up, then begin to register where she was, what day this was, and what matters she had to tend to today. The process of practical stock-taking complete, her mind would then enter some uncomfortable furrows she would have liked to avoid. She could almost feel her neurons slipping into these ruts, and for a few more seconds it would be a bumpy ride. She had been following this pattern long enough now to know that any attempt to get back to sleep was futile, and that lying awake in bed was only going to result in more mental ruts. Whenever this happened, she would unwind herself from the pretzel-shaped position her body ended up in while she slept, swing her legs over the edge of the bed, and rise.

Since she had begun living alone, watching television news had become an essential part of Azita's morning routine. She felt comforted by the lighthearted tone of the news anchors, the playful comments they made to one another, the lilt in their voices as they delivered the lurid details about local tragedies, the way these news items were interspersed with bright advertisements for breakfast foods and hygiene products. The content of the early morning programs provoked a mixture of amusement and revulsion in her that she enjoyed, and this feeling helped set the tone for the day ahead.

There was a distant sound of thunder this Saturday morning. She lay in bed for longer than usual, her mind churning and her body switching from one tense position to another. When she finally got up, the first glimmer of daylight was just appearing beyond her window, and she could hear the distant chirping of birds. She pulled on a sweatshirt and some socks, padded into the living room and turned the television on, then went into the kitchen to make her tea. While the tea was brewing, she sat down on the couch and stared absently at the screen, which was tuned to CNN. During the weather forecast, she leaned her head back against the couch and closed her eyes.

When she opened them again, she was surprised to see that the time at the bottom of the screen read 8:03. She was even more surprised by the realization that what had woken her had been the chime of a doorbell. It was a sound she didn't hear often, and at first, she thought it might be part of the television program. Then she heard it again, and this time the synthetic arpeggio of the chime rose clearly above the buzz emanating from the television.

Someone was actually at the door. It took a few seconds for her to process this fact, and once she did, she found she couldn't move. She wasn't frightened, exactly—fear wasn't really part of her nature. Instead, what she felt was a sense of anticipation, as if this chime were somehow laden with meaning. She got up from the couch, ran her fingers through her long black hair, and moved slowly toward the door.

She shouldn't have been shocked to see Ethan standing in her doorway, because she had known he would show up sooner or later. There had been something urgent in his tone when he requested her number at the end of the only conversation they'd ever had. No cell phones had been allowed at the center where she met him, so she had written her address and phone number on a piece of cardboard she tore from a donut box. When she extended her hand to give the information to him, he grabbed it and enclosed it between his huge, trembling fists, locked her in a stare, and asked, "Can I visit you when I get out?"

Azita hadn't felt threatened by his brazen self-invitation, even though it came out of nowhere. His tone was imploring, but somehow innocent, like the tone a child might use when asking for another bedtime story. His hands tightened around hers until the pressure was almost uncomfortable, and he looked into her eyes for what felt like a very long time, with no trace of a leer. Azita felt a surge of emotion she didn't recognize, something akin to tenderness. "Of course," she answered. She took the piece of cardboard back from him and scribbled her street address on it. When she returned it, she seized his hand and shook it gently, suggesting that a pact had been made.

Now Ethan was standing in her doorway, and the first thing Azita noticed was that he was very tall. She remembered this vaguely, but it was shocking to see now that he filled the entire height of the door frame. The second thing she noticed was that it was raining outside; it surprised her that she had not heard the rain until now.

Ethan was drenched, which meant he had been standing outside for some time before making the decision to ring the bell. A rivulet of water was making its way down from the crown of his head, and Azita watched it slip into the corner of his eye socket and wind gently down his nose.

It was unclear who would speak first. Ethan lifted his arm and swiped it across his nose and mouth, then shook his head slightly the way a dog might, spraying droplets in Azita's direction. "Sorry, I'm soaked," he said. "It's really pounding out here."

As she looked up at his face, it dawned on her that she had not retained a clear memory of it at all; she might not have recognized him if she had encountered him somewhere besides in her doorway. She did remember the scruffy beard because he had put a fine point on it when it had been his turn to speak at the support group session. "Yeah, I'm wearing this Hezbollah beard," he had said, "but I'm not a terrorist, I promise." He turned in Azita's direction and smiled when he said this, and she knew that the comment was meant specifically for her. No one else in that circle would have gotten the reference.

Azita was not easily flustered, nor was she shy, nor was she one to come undone in the presence of a man, even if he was tall, and—she now noticed—had a chiseled, perfectly symmetrical face that seemed to belong to a department store mannequin or G.I. Joe doll.

"Ethan, right?" she said, although she knew perfectly well who he was, and she knew that he knew she did. "I mean, I know who you are. I'm just a bit surprised to see you. When did you get out?"

"Early this morning. I got an Uber and came straight here. I told my parents not to expect me until Monday."

"Oh," Azita said. It occurred to her, as she turned and led him into her apartment, that today was Saturday, which meant that Monday was two nights away. The thought also crossed her mind that Ethan had been in Ridgemont for over a year, which meant he had not touched or been touched by a woman during that time.

She stopped in the middle of the living room and looked back at him. He had taken only a few steps inside the apartment and had left the door gaping open, the rain falling in a sheet behind him. She skirted past him and closed it while he remained standing still at the edge of the room.

"Nice place," he said when she turned to face him. "How do you afford this on a teacher's salary?"

"My parents. Pre-revolutionary feudal system money, remember?"

He chuckled. During the brief speech she had made the night she met him, at the one and only support group she had ever attended, she had revealed a few details about her family background: how her Iranian grandfather had accumulated an obscene amount of money as a landholding pistachio producer under the Shah; how the money had been secured in Swiss bank accounts before the Islamic Revolution came; how her father, aunts, and uncles had safely relocated to the States before the shit hit the proverbial fan.

"Hey, it's not your fault," Ethan had said at the circle.

Now he said it again. "It's not your fault, remember?" He paused for a minute and looked at her, then continued. "You should see where I grew up. My father, in addition to whatever shady business he conducts, is the deacon of the Holy Spirit Catholic Church. Did I tell you that before? I keep asking him how he can reconcile living in a million-dollar house with 'blessed are the meek' and the rich man and the camel passing through the eye of a needle and all that shit, but he's got this argument about how the church needs to be wealthy in order to do its good works. At least he's not a pedophile. As far as I know. Just brainwashed. He's what I call a Fox News Catholic."

His words had come out in a torrent, and when he finished speaking Azita realized that she had been staring at him, so entranced by the expression in his eyes and the movements of his mouth that she had barely taken in what he said. He had a permanently astonished look about him that reminded her of the pet rabbit she had as a child.

"Sit down, sit down," she muttered.

He chose the most uncomfortable chair in the room, a straight-backed leather Carver chair that her parents had bought her and that she had always hated. She wanted to suggest he sit on the couch instead, but she thought he might misinterpret the suggestion. Feeling awkward, she remained standing.

"Cool rug," Ethan said, looking down at the Persian carpet that covered the entire floor of the living room.

"Thanks. It's been in my family for years, since my dad was a kid. It was probably made by a young girl, maybe as young as seven or eight. Most rugs were woven by children back then—by girls, that is. Now I think they make a lot of them by machine. It comes from a little village outside Arak, the town where my father grew up."

"Not to be confused with *I-raq*," said Ethan, pronouncing the name of the country correctly. "Isn't Arak where they're supposedly manufacturing all the nuclear weapons now?"

Azita couldn't hide her surprise. "That's right! I'm impressed."

"I guess it's supposed to be some kind of secret underground facility. Except it couldn't be that big a secret if I know about it, right?"

She smiled at him, then moved over to the couch and seated herself on the end closest to the Carver chair. They sat in silence for a few minutes. The rain had grown weaker, and the sound of the television pushed itself forward into the room. They turned toward the large, flat screen at the same time, where CNN was replaying the footage from the angry, torch-bearing mob that had gathered in Charlottesville the previous night. The sound grew louder as the mob began to chant in unison, "You will not replace us! You will not replace us!"

Azita had seen the news about the rally last night but had somehow managed to erase the images of the mob from her mind. Not wanting to repeat the feeling of nausea she'd felt then, she picked up the remote and muted the sound. "We can keep it on if you want," she said, "but I'd really rather not hear their disgusting voices."

"Yeah, I agree," Ethan said. He shifted his body away from the television. "So, tell me about your job," he said.

His eyes had found hers. She felt the same swell of tenderness and trust she had felt when she had met him at the center. "God, you really don't want to hear about that!"

"Oh, but I do. I'm guessing your school is a lot like the one I went to. I'm trying to picture what it's like for all those hormonal eighth-grade boys having someone like you at the front of the classroom."

"All those *privileged* hormonal eighth-grade boys, you mean. I'm not a woman to them—I'm barely a person. They just think of me as part of the help."

"I seriously doubt that."

Ethan's face flushed and he dropped his eyes. Sensing that he was embarrassed by the direction of the conversation, she tried to pivot. "*Lord of the Flies* is always the most popular book I teach, especially with the boys. There are no women in it besides that sow they kill."

"You mean *rape* and kill," he said.

"Right," she replied with a chuckle.

They chatted idly for a while, and the conversation grew so easy and natural that Azita almost forgot he was a guest. Suddenly remembering her Iranian manners, she rose from the couch and put her hand on Ethan's shoulder. "Can I get you some tea?"

He answered her question with a question. "You got any alcohol?"

Serving alcohol in the morning to a man she barely knew should have made Azita uncomfortable, but somehow it didn't. She watched him in fascination from behind the kitchen door as she made him a screwdriver. His long, lean body was inclined again toward the television screen, and his huge hands gripped the chair arms. He reminded her of the El Greco painting of Cardinal Guevara, the Grand Inquisitor, that had been the subject of an entire lecture in one of her undergraduate art history classes. Her professor's thesis had been that El Greco was one of the first painters to fully explore the psychological potential of portraiture, and that he had used the subtle detail of the Cardinal's clenched left fist to indicate his inner turmoil.

Everything about Ethan, from his tensed muscles to his rapt expression as he stared at the screen, suggested intensity. The light from the screen flickered gently across his prominent cheekbones. He's beautiful, Azita thought. But he's fucked up.

⟡

Azita didn't like to admit to herself that she might be a bit fucked up too. But why else would she have willfully attended a support group, the one where she had met Ethan just a few months ago?

There was no immediate precipitating factor that led her to Ridgemont Psychiatric Center—at least not one that she could single out. As a youth she'd had a few cutting episodes, so she supposed there had been something wrong with her for a while. She had kept these episodes carefully hidden from her parents, whose trust in their daughter was wholehearted and unquestioning. When her mother found the jagged bottom of a Coke can under her bed, Azita pretended she was using the can for a school project, and her mother accepted the explanation. Lying in her bed the night after the discovery, Azita had been plagued with guilt. If her parents had ever known she was digging the Coke can into her own thighs and drawing blood, they would have been devastated and bewildered.

The cutting episodes belonged to a stage of Azita's life she now looked back on dispassionately, but the restlessness inside her had only grown stronger. At times it felt more like anger than restlessness, and it frustrated her that she couldn't find a concrete subject on which to pin it. She had entertained many theories about this over the years, some of them extravagant, some twisted, some simplistic, and some full of psychology mumbo-jumbo.

Growing up Iranian in the American South, Azita had always felt like a fish out of water in both communities. Although she had grown up in the bosom of the Atlanta Iranian community, a group so insular that it often didn't seem like part of the United States at all, she didn't feel much kinship with most Iranians. The topics the younger generation of Iranians talked about were ones that Azita could not weigh in on. The men her age usually talked about computer science or engineering or one of the other practical subjects they inevitably chose to study. The women talked about a variety of subjects, but hair and makeup always found their way into the conversation. In general, there was little substance for Azita to sink her teeth into.

The decision to go to a support group was not one she thought about carefully; it was made on the spur of the moment one morning. She had woken up that morning at 4:17, as usual, and her thoughts had started to go down the same paths they often went down: her difficulty with relationships, her detachment from her Iranian family, her inability to pin down her cultural identity, her constant sense of not belonging. But this time, they led her to scary places: to vivid visions of extreme self-harm. Instead of getting out of bed and beginning her morning rituals, she continued to lie there, paralyzed by panic. Her heart raced, her muscles tensed, and her skin burned. When she finally got out of bed and realized several hours had gone by, she reached for her phone and began to search for help.

The literature on Ridgemont Psychiatric Center's website promised an "individualized approach" guided by "licensed medical experts" and "qualified professionals" who understood that "every client is unique." The treatment plan did not include any medications, and this appealed to Azita, who had never been interested in drugs. But Ridgemont was impossibly expensive, and she certainly wasn't going to ask her parents for the money. She decided she would attend one of the free support groups and take it from there.

She chose a session called "Emotions Anonymous," which sounded broad enough to encompass whatever her unidentified problems might be. But as soon as she sat down, she realized that she didn't belong in this group at all. Among the participants were a middle-aged woman with long, stringy hair who couldn't seem to stop the frantic shaking of her legs, a younger woman with multiple piercings who scowled at Azita when she sat down, and a frighteningly thin, careworn man whose very appearance freaked her out.

Ethan entered the room after the others were seated and introduced himself as a "volunteer" who lived at the facility and would be leading tonight's session. He presented a brief synopsis of his own life before turning his attention to the participants, and from this Azita had gleaned the following: he was thirty-three years old; he had grown up in Atlanta's wealthy Buckhead community; he had been raised to be a devout Catholic; he had begun a degree in theater arts from Columbia but dropped out to go to Haiti on a mission trip; he had experienced a serious crisis of faith while there; he had subsequently gotten "messed up" and had checked himself into the center in order to "put himself back together." He explained all of this in a rapid-fire speech during which, in addition to the reference to Hezbollah, he also made references to Beckett and Anouilh. These references, too, were lost on all the participants but Azita.

His arms were covered with scars, some deep and purple, some elongated and protruding. He was obviously making no attempt to hide them, since he wore a muscle shirt, but he offered no explanation for them either. Azita didn't ask where the scars came from, and no one else did either. But when Ethan approached her at the refreshment table after the meeting, he volunteered the information.

"In case you're wondering, these are mostly cigarette burns," he said. "It's a long story, but it has to do with poking my nose in where it didn't belong."

"I wasn't wondering," she answered. "But thanks for sharing anyway."

"Maybe I'll tell you about them one of these days," he whispered.

എ

After his fourth screwdriver and her second, they found themselves seated on the Persian rug with their backs against the couch. Ethan took a long sip of his drink and then looked at her with a challenge in his eyes.

"Okay, so I need to know why someone like you, with your looks, your brains, and your money, ends up in an EA support group."

Although it was obvious that the question was a serious one, Azita, who was feeling a bit lightheaded, chose to answer him teasingly. "I think it goes back to the moment of my conception. I was conceived during an Iraqi bombing raid on Tehran. There were almost nightly bombing raids back then, and my parents, who were newlyweds at the time, had to go down to the basement all the time to take cover. On the night I was conceived, the bombing raid was really intense, and I guess the fear must have stoked my parents' passion."

"I don't quite follow," said Ethan. "How does being conceived in a basement lead to a support group thirty years later?"

"I don't know. I guess I was born angry. As you know, those Iraqi bombs that almost killed my parents were manufactured by the US, like most of the bombs in the world. When my mom first told me the story as a child, I remember feeling a sense of panic at the thought that my parents might have died, and I might never have come into being. But when I thought about it later, after I understood where babies came from, I started seeing my parents as anti-imperialist heroes. Even the sperm and the egg had fought valiantly against the evil American empire—the 'Great Satan,' as they call it in Iran. Anger is almost a part of my DNA."

Ethan looked thoughtful. "I think your theory contains a glaring contradiction. The way I look at it, you should be grateful for American military might. You owe your very existence to it."

"You've got a point," she responded. "Maybe the damage came later, like when I was tormented by my classmates in school."

She said this lightly, but Ethan scanned her face with genuine concern and reached over to touch her arm. "Do tell," he said.

Azita wasn't sure where to begin. "It probably started in middle school," she said. "I attended a public middle school in Cobb County, at the time when they had those stickers inside of science textbooks announcing that evolution was just a theory. Remember those? Anyway, I didn't fit in. I was a visible minority, which didn't help. I guess I was just an easy target. It didn't matter that I had only lived the first year of my life in Iran, and that after my parents fled to Atlanta I had only visited occasionally during the summer. It didn't matter that I had grown up in Georgia or that I was much more comfortable speaking English than Farsi. In Cobb County in the nineties, it was enough just to look Middle Eastern and to have a foreign name."

"Obviously. I'm sure you stuck out all over the place. And the boys might have ridiculed you, but secretly, they probably all had the hots for you."

The playfulness of this remark made her realize that anger was beginning to spill out of her, and she wondered if this might be Ethan's way of trying to lighten the conversation. What was it about this near stranger that made her want to fling open her emotional floodgates? She probably shouldn't trust him so completely, but now that she'd started, she wasn't sure how to stop.

"Actually, it was mostly the girls who tormented me," she said. Here she paused and thought back on the incidents of bullying in middle school. A lot of it was about the food her mother packed her for lunch, which was almost always Persian. One time her lunch was ghormeh sabzi, her favorite Iranian stew made of spinach, fenugreek, and dark red beans. A blonde girl sitting next to her in the cafeteria watched in horror as she opened her lunchbox, then asked her if someone had thrown up in there. Everyone at the table laughed, including some girls she had thought of as friends. A few days later, she pulled her lunchbox out in the cafeteria and was surprised to find a note inside. Someone had sketched a crude skull and crossbones on it, and beneath it were the words "POISON: ISLAM FOOD."

The memory of these incidents made tears well up in Azita's eyes, and for a moment, she couldn't speak. She looked over at Ethan and saw the softness in his expression, and again she was struck by his beauty. He was waiting for her to continue, so she found her voice.

"When I was in high school, the bullying came from all sides— boys, girls, even teachers. After 9/11, it was mostly political branding. One of my best friends from childhood looked at me one day out of the blue and asked why I didn't wear a headscarf. A boy from my math class approached me at my locker one morning and snarled, 'Hey, didn't I just see you on TV last night shouting 'Death to America?' The social studies teacher turned to me in the middle of class one day and said, 'I sure hope you will stand up during the Pledge of Allegiance, Azita. Because that flag stands for freedom.'"

"Hahaha. Right. Freedom," Ethan laughed. "Who was it who

said *freedom for the pike is death for the minnows?*"

Azita closed her eyes, the memory bitter. She had just entered tenth grade when the World Trade Center came crashing down. Like any other American that September, she had found it impossible to tear herself away from the haunting images: the planes slicing through the glistening windows of the towers as though they were made of paper; the dazed and horrified people on the streets; the ghastly gray smoke; the bodies falling through the air in slow motion against an obscenely blue sky. She was spellbound by the vicarious sense of heroism and courage, utterly engulfed by the collective consciousness. She wanted to share in the grief and horror of her classmates and teachers, but they wouldn't let her in.

Ethan touched her arm again. "Sorry. Didn't mean to jump in there," he said.

Azita shook her head. "It's fine. I was just remembering. When I was in eleventh grade, I went with an American friend named Betsy to a Fourth of July picnic at Stone Mountain. Before the fireworks began, they projected this video on the granite outcropping. It was the usual patriotic message about the brave men and women in uniform who fight for our freedom, blah blah blah—but this time, instead of a bunch of soldiers smiling and cradling foreign-looking children in their arms, it was totally militaristic, with these attractive male and female soldiers dressed in sparkling uniforms, flying airplanes, saluting, and marching with their weapons up. I turned to Betsy and asked her to explain how, exactly, killing Afghan, Iraqi, and Pakistani civilians gave us freedom. I was genuinely interested in the answer, but she just stared at me as though she didn't understand the question."

Ethan stroked her arm, and Azita bit her cheek. She didn't feel comfortable telling Ethan what she was now remembering: that during her senior year in high school, she had found herself sucked into the sordid world of teenage sex. Maybe it was a desperate attempt to fit in. Maybe she was trying to deaden her senses so she wouldn't notice how hurt she was. Maybe it was payback for all the insults she had suffered. Whatever the reason was, she threw herself fully into the meat market of girl-boy relationships. One morning at school, a veritable posse of girls surrounded her as she navigated the hallway on her way to class. She didn't remember the exact words spoken— perhaps she had blotted them out of her memory—but the gist was that she shouldn't mess with any of the American boys and should stick with Aladdin or Sinbad. At least they could have gotten her ethnicity right, she remembered thinking.

The memory of this incident pushed a button, and her words came pouring out. "You know, I did have boyfriends in high school— like, lots of them. This did not earn me the right kind of popularity in school, and it definitely didn't help my reputation in the Iranian community, where I was branded as a slut. Which was outrageous and unfair, of course. Many of the older Iranian men I know have been involved in extra-marital affairs, and the younger men always feel like predators to me. Iranian women usually fall into one of two camps—they're either appallingly subservient to their husbands or repulsively flirtatious and needy of male attention."

She caught herself here, categorizing these women the same way her classmates had categorized her.

"The truth is," she continued, "I'm not in a position to pass judgment on anyone's relationships, because most of mine have been unhealthy ones. For some reason, I was always attracted to damaged guys, and the relationships never ended well. There was Mike, the self-involved substance abuser. There was Adam, the spoiled mama's boy who wanted me as arm candy. There was Jeff, the good-hearted loser it took me months to get rid of. Then there was Justin, the handsome Jamaican hip-hop artist who was four years younger than me.

He went into a tailspin after we broke up, and that's when I realized I was starting to lose my sense of self. After that, I swore off men."

They sat in silence for a few moments. In the void, Azita's eyes drifted back to the TV. A line of riot police, their shields raised, pulsated in front of her. The street around them was hazy with smoke, and chaos was visible behind it: protesters being pummeled and pushed, struggling to get up from the ground. The words at the bottom of the screen read BREAKING NEWS: TWO INJURED IN VIOLENT CLASHES.

Sitting beside Ethan on the rug, Azita could feel him shaking his head gently.

"Should I turn it off?" Azita asked.

"Nah, leave it on. It's a great backdrop for our conversation."

"Okay," Azita said, though she wasn't at all sure what he meant. Her legs were stretched out in front of her, and she shifted them slightly, revealing a tattoo on her calf.

"Hey, what's that?" Ethan asked.

"It's a pterodactyl," Azita answered. "It was a stupid affectation at age fifteen. I think I was just trying to piss off my parents. And all those Bible-thumpers I went to school with, who believed in talking snakes in the Garden of Eden but weren't sure that dinosaurs were real."

Ethan lifted his T-shirt, then removed it altogether and tossed it on the couch behind him. "I designed mine too," he said. "I think I was in my twenties, but I had some grandiose ideas back then."

Azita leaned in close to examine the tattoo, which was right in the center of Ethan's chest. The intricate design featured gnarled, thorny vines with what looked like a mushroom cloud rising above them. Beneath this design was a black rectangle with a simple statement inside it in white lettering: *LIVE TO THE POINT OF TEARS.* Below the quote was the name of its author, Albert Camus.

"Corny, I know," Ethan said. He didn't quite slur the words, but

Azita could tell his tongue was becoming loose. She reached over and stroked the tattoo gently, then moved her fingers down Ethan's chest and brought them to rest on his left forearm. She massaged his scars a few times, then lifted her eyes to his face.

"So, are you ready to tell me about these?"

Ethan brushed her fingers away and began massaging the scars himself. "It happened on a mission trip to Haiti." He paused, and when he spoke again, his voice came out in a whisper. "There was this one girl. She was a child—only thirteen. I never even saw her more than a few times, but every time I did, she smiled at me. She had an amazing smile, really innocent and sincere. I tried to save her—not in the Christian sense, not save her soul—just save her from being taken away and, you know, sold. It was unbelievable how all the mission people there just pretended like the whole thing wasn't happening. They pay thousands of dollars to go on those mission trips, and yeah, they work a few hours a day on food, water, and shelter stuff. But it's mostly a photo opportunity. Lots of selfies with little dark-skinned children to post on Facebook."

"I think you're digressing."

"Oh, sorry. So when I realized what was happening with the girl—her name was Nathalie, but I didn't know that until later—I got involved. Too involved."

He shook his head vigorously from side to side as if to stop himself before another torrent came pouring out. Azita noticed that a few small tears were forming in the corners of his eyes.

She tried to change the subject. "Since when are Catholics so political?" she asked. "I thought you guys only worried about abortion."

"You think I compare killing a collection of cells to killing living, breathing schoolchildren? What kind of idiot do you take me for?"

"I mean, I just assumed that if you went on a mission trip—"

"That was just my ticket in. I had some notion that I would be able to do something real in Haiti. But then I got mixed up with the wrong people. Anyway, I was never on a mission for Jesus, even though I guess I had some kind of messianic thing going on."

Azita shifted her body slightly until her right leg was touching his left one. "How about now? Are you still trying to save the world, or did your time at Ridgemont cure you of that?"

"It's kind of hard to save the world when you're taking mega-doses of lithium."

"Are you still taking it?"

Ethan ignored her question and didn't look at her when he spoke again. "What's really fucked up is that Fox News Catholics are all warmongers these days. They listen to assholes like Dinesh D'Souza, even though everything about him flies in the face of what Jesus supposedly preached. Do you know what the Catholic doctrine of 'just war' is? It basically means that God is telling Christians who to kill. I don't see how that's different from Muslims believing that Allah told them they should fly into the World Trade Center."

Throughout his impassioned speech, Azita watched his bare torso in fascination. His shoulders lifted and rose as he spoke, and his whole upper body rippled in a way that made her want to touch it—to peel back his skin and study it so she could figure out how he was put together.

After a brief pause, he continued, his tone now turning lighter. "Besides, there's all that stuff about sex for procreation only. It's as if they're afraid of their own bodies, like they think they're dirty or something. Original sin? Give me a break. We were doing just fine in Greece and Rome. Yeah, maybe they had slavery, but all those or-gies! And then along came those Inquisition assholes with their guilt and their sordid view of human nature and plunged us into the Dark Ages. I don't think we've emerged yet."

Azita's head was swimming now—she wasn't sure whether it was the alcohol, the story Ethan had told her, or the feel of his large body next to hers. Even sitting on the floor, he towered over her. She rested her head against his chest and closed her eyes.

She couldn't be sure how long she slept, but when she drifted out of her doze, Ethan's eyes were riveted on the television screen. She lifted her head from his chest and sat up. Still feeling dizzy, she leaned her back against the couch, then turned to see what he was looking at. It took her a minute to process the scene that was being shown repeatedly: a small gray-green car backing rapidly down a narrow street, plowing straight into the crowd.

"What the hell is going on in this country?" Ethan said. His voice was soft, but Azita could feel the intensity behind it. "What the fuck is wrong with people?"

She got up to refill their drinks, and they sipped them as they stared at the screen. The sound was muted, but the images repeated before their eyes: the car plowing into the crowd, the crumpled bodies of the injured protesters strewn on the street, the stunned faces of the eyewitnesses giving their accounts, and finally, the smiling face of the young murder victim flashing across the screen. At intervals they spoke, and a few times, they dozed. At some point Azita got up to refill their drinks again, but soon they abandoned them. Glasses half full of melting ice sat on the floor in front of them.

When Trump came on the screen to deliver his address from his golf club in Bedminster, Azita picked up her cell phone and checked the time. 3:34 PM. How long had it been since the car had sped backward into the crowd? Time did not make sense right now. Was it today Ethan had shown up on her doorstep?

They sat with their arms locked together and watched Trump approach the podium. Azita didn't want to hear his voice, but she picked up the remote and turned up the sound. "We condemn in the strongest possible terms this egregious display of hatred, bigotry, and violence," he said. Then after a pause, he added, "On many sides. On *many* sides."

Ethan tightened his grip on Azita's arm, and she leaned against his chest. While Trump spoke, Ethan's ragged breathing echoed in her ears, drowning out all but the key phrases: *incredible veterans... great people... terrible events... swift restoration of law and order... protection of innocent lives.* Ethan remained mostly silent during the speech, muttering only an occasional comment that reverberated up from his chest and into her head. When Trump said children should be able to "go outside and play or be with their parents and have a good time," Ethan whispered, "You bet, Donnie! Let's all go out and have a good time!" When Trump talked about the need to *come together with true affection for each other*, he mumbled, "Yep. True affection. That's what this is about."

The speech took a turn, and Trump started touting the achievements of his administration. Forgetting that Azita's head was resting against his chest, Ethan sat up to shout at the screen, "Unemployment figures, you fucking asshole? Car companies and trade deals? Wanna tell that to the mother of the woman who just got mowed down?" He shook his head as if to clear it, then leaned back again and reached for Azita. "I'm sorry," he said. "He just pushes a button. I mean, can you see that glint in his eye? It's not just me, right? He totally *loves* this."

Azita wasn't sure how to answer. Ethan clutched Azita's hand as they both listened to Trump delivering the usual platitudes: "No matter our color, creed, religion, or political party, we are all Americans first. We love our country. We love our God."

Now Ethan shot up from the floor and lunged toward the television, using his finger like a weapon to point at Trump's image. "*Our* God?" he shouted. "Our *GOD*? That's a good one, Donnie! Oh boy, I bet the Fox News Catholics are eating this up! They're all sitting in their living rooms right now watching this on their big-screen TVs and talking about all those socialists and dark masses who are trying to take the country away from 'real' Americans. Real Americans like Jesus, right?"

He let out an unusual sound, a cross between a cackle and a wail. Then he began singing in a voice so full-bodied and gorgeous that it gave Azita the chills:

> We've got the American Jesus
> See him on the interstate
> We've got the American Jesus
> He helped build the president's estate

He paused now and looked down at Azita, who was staring up at him, dumbfounded. "Ever hear that song?" he asked her. "It's from before our time, but it's a good one. I used to play it just to piss my parents off." He cackled again, then began waving his arms madly through the air, shouting, "Jesus! Jesus, where *are* you? Where'd you go? Are you on *vacation*?"

Azita reached up, seized one of his waving arms, and pulled him down toward her. He sat down on the rug and leaned back against the couch.

"Shhh," she whispered, stroking his arm. "Calm down, dude."

She began to massage his burn marks gently, and she could feel his breath growing deeper and slower. Then she clasped one of his enormous hands and slid it up inside her T-shirt, across her smooth abdomen and toward her breasts. As he eased her body backward and lowered his own on top of it, the Persian rug beneath her felt as soft and yielding as a cloud.

DYING IN AMERICA

SINA'S HUSBAND, AZIZ, DIED on a morning in March. His life was simply over, suddenly and irrevocably, like the dropping and breaking of a teacup.

She had not expected him to die on the morning he died. No one had expected it. There was no mounting evidence to suggest that his death was imminent, no single precipitating factor, no traceable chain of cause and effect. Even in hindsight, it was difficult to settle upon a satisfactory explanation.

They were gathered together for Now Ruz in the family home in California on the night before it happened: Sina, Aziz, their son and daughter, and their three grandchildren. His final night on this earth was imprinted in each of their minds in a series of images that had the clarity and precision of videos across a screen. They could not have known, as they stored these images away, that they were destined to play them over and over, with varying sequence and intensity, for such a long time to come.

It was odd how dissimilar and disconnected their images were. The oldest grandson, Kamran, had helped his grandfather into the shower that evening and would forever picture the scar on his chest, a remnant of his bypass surgery. Although the surgery had taken place several years before, the scar, which was two inches wide and bright pink, looked fresh and alive—angry. Kamran had known the scar existed but was shocked and disturbed to see it at such close range. Long after the ordeal, whenever he attempted to picture his grandfather, the image that pushed itself forward was of the sunken and scarred chest.

The final image that Ariane, the adolescent granddaughter, would record of her grandfather was tinged with guilt. He was sitting on the couch, and she was passing in and out of the room with a cell phone in her hand. Each time she passed through, her grandfather tried to get her attention with an affectionate verbal jab, but she smiled politely and continued talking. She had tried to hide her annoyance, but after he died it occurred to her that it had emanated from her and that he had surely felt it.

For the youngest grandson, Ali, who was five, the final image of his grandfather was an eerily tender one: the old man was calling him forward, asking him to remove his wool hat—the one he had worn for as long as the child could remember—and demanding a kiss on the top of his bald head. His grandfather had taught him the Farsi word for hat: kola. For months to come, he would continually replay the sound of his grandfather's voice uttering the word kola and would simultaneously relive the sensation of his own lips on his grandfather's cold, hairless head.

Jamshid, the son, would not retain a concrete image of his father on the night before he died. Instead, he would dwell on his own behavior that night—his excessive drinking, his erratic mood, and his furtive escapes to the dark basement where he kept his stash of marijuana and his bong.

The daughter, Roshan, recorded an incoherent mixture of sound and image: the awkward way her father looked as he sat on the couch with his bird-thin legs defensively crossed beneath him; the blaring of the television set at which he stared blankly; the disorder in the kitchen where the dinner was being haphazardly prepared between drinks; the cacophony of voices which failed to form meaning.

For Sina herself, five decades of marriage coalesced into a single terrifying image of her husband when she last saw him fully alive, sitting hunched over on a couch. This image was accompanied by the echo of his repeated and increasingly querulous demands for another glass of vodka. As always, she had protested half-heartedly, and then complied.

Wife, daughter, son, grandchildren—all would replay the sound of his voice traveling across the house from the room where they had abandoned him. He shouted out to them—but then, after he realized they were on another wavelength, he began to mutter to himself. His tone was plaintive, then sarcastic, then hostile, then desperate—and finally, barely audible.

And then, of course, the sudden image of his fallen body on the living room floor, his forehead bloodied and his legs twisted awkwardly to one side. When Jamshid lifted him from the floor and carried him to the bedroom, the role reversal was shocking, incomprehensible.

And next, the springing into action: the mustering of sobriety, the perfunctory family council and the collective decision to avoid the emergency room, the expeditious trip to CVS to buy gauze and peroxide and butterfly clamps, the gentle dressing of the wound, the delicate removal of shoes and belt and trademark hat and newly purchased jeans and cowboy shirt, the slipping on of the pajamas without which he could not sleep, the careful arrangement of the pillows around the injured head.

And after he was safely in bed, the heedless, empty continuation of merriment: the repetition of jokes everyone already knew, the corny songs dredged up from decades past, the giggles and cackles and croons, the indifferent rise in volume in one room while in the next room he silently descended.

And finally, Sina's voice in the half-light uttering the simplest, yet most important sentence she had ever uttered: "Children, I think your father is dying."

It was not until after they had rubbed their swollen eyes and massaged their pounding temples and heaved their sodden bodies out of bed that the stark reality of their mother's statement dawned on them. Only then did they recall the scene of Baba's crumpled body on the floor and begin, groggily, to connect that picture to the words that drifted together from the tiny, pathetic sound of their mother's voice.

He was not dead when they came into the room, and he was not dead when they called the ambulance—on the contrary, he burst forth with sudden venomous lucidity.

"It's just an abrasion! Just an abrasion!" he sputtered. He was not dead when the paramedic ripped open his pajama shirt and listened to his failing heart.

"Who are you?" he snarled at the grotesque crewcut figure leaning over him with a stethoscope. "Where did you get your medical degree?"

He was alive enough to notice the rolls of fat bulging beneath the paramedic's uniform, alive enough to smell the mixture of coffee and ketchup on his breath. He was still alive when they strapped him to the gurney and drove him away.

There must have been a precise moment, as in all deaths, when his life ended—when the impact hit and the teacup shattered. But the clocks in the hospital where he died continued their dutiful, omniscient ticking throughout the event, without a discernible pause or a rise or fall in pitch or volume. The nurses and technicians moved through the hospital rooms soundlessly, as they had been trained to do in such moments. They spoke in whispers and adopted other-worldly expressions to suit the occasion. It was pronounced: "He is dead." The death certificate was signed and submitted, and their work was over. Everything was clean, professional, and appropriate.

∾

Greenlawn Cemetery is a sprawling oasis wedged between a gas station and a Walmart on one end and a liquor store and car dealership on the other. The green grass the cemetery's name promises is incongruously lush, considering the asphalt that encroaches upon it from all sides. Flowers of every season and clime bloom simultaneously in a garish effusion of color, and stone angels and flags intermingle in the solemn duty of watching over the dead. The literature of Greenlawn Cemetery does not lie when it claims to tailor-make its burials to suit the wishes of the bereaved family: Muslims and Hindus and Catholics and Protestants have all been accommodated there and lie peacefully side by side.

The funeral director was polite and solicitous; he had performed every imaginable kind of rite, he assured them, and he understood and respected their desires. He even provided, free of charge, a temporary marker to place over the mound and donated a bouquet of plastic geraniums—a favorite, he knew, among Muslims—to place in the complementary vase.

He was wrapped in a shroud and the simple pine box that served as his casket was hinged on one side so that his body could fall into the earth according to Muslim custom. And so Sina's husband died, and so he was buried.

∾

But Sina knew that this was not his death: not the alternating drunkenness and hilarity and confusion and neglect and solitude of his final night; not the hematoma from his fall against the wooden chest; not the failure to take him to an emergency room; not the hour and minute and second recorded on his death certificate; not even the suffocation of dirt and the covering over with grass and plastic.

As Aziz's body tumbled into the earth, Sina had the sensation that he was tumbling not down, but backward through time. The teacup that was his life had fallen through another part of the space-time continuum—a part that defied ticking clocks and death certificates and numerical measurements. He had been falling toward death for a long time—forever, it seemed.

He had probably begun to die a few years earlier, she thought. Perhaps it was when he first started to feel that his children no longer understood him, or even heard him; when he began to feel irrelevant; when he retired and his status as a brilliant doctor no longer carried weight; when he first looked in the mirror and saw how hollow his eyes had become; when he began to need assistance to get into or out of a car.

But in her heart, she knew that his death began earlier than that. He had begun to die years and years ago, maybe as far back as the time when the children had defied his wishes and decided to pursue impractical degrees in philosophy and literature, when they boasted of their alternative sexual practices, when they brought home blond "partners" whose English even his non-native ears detected as improper.

It was even possible, she thought, that he had begun to die earlier still, during the children's adolescent years, when they insisted on dragging him to Yosemite and Yellowstone and the Grand Canyon, declaring these places to be the most beautiful on earth, when they had never seen the Alborz and Zagros Mountains, the windswept plains of Khuzestan, or the Great Salt Lake of Urmia. She remembered, with a stab of guilt, how they had blared rap music in the car while driving with their father through landscapes that were foreign to him but that must surely have reminded him of home.

Had he begun dying even earlier than that, perhaps as early as their preteen years? They had been determined during those years to fly in the face of his notions of propriety; had insisted on wearing faded jeans with deliberate holes in them, dyeing their hair blue and pink, and walking with a gait that to him seemed both weak and aggressive, decidedly American. This, Sina thought, must surely have contributed to his decline.

Or perhaps it was even earlier, when they turned away from Farsi, the rich and beautiful language of their ancestors, speaking it badly and reluctantly and adopting American accents. For much of their childhood, their father's elegant Farsi was muffled, even to his own ears, by the nasal sounds of their American English.

Did he begin to die as a much younger man? Could his death have begun when Sina insisted that they leave Iran to live in the United States and raise their children there? Could her own acquisition of American habits—walking barefoot, letting her fingernails get dirty, refusing to go to the hair salon, wearing shorts and T-shirts, laughing loudly with her head thrown back—could these behaviors have begun to kill him?

But as she sprinkled dirt over her husband's grave, Sina's mind shifted back to the forward position. She had no regrets. Her children had done what any child—indeed, any living thing—will do when forced to adjust to a new environment: they had developed survival techniques. They had become chameleons, changing their colors to blend in, to avoid being noticed and targeted. They had grown up to be fine people, and although it was foreign to them and they felt no allegiance to it, they had a healthy respect for the country of their parents' birth.

No, it was not possible to pinpoint her husband's death, although Sina knew she would never stop trying. She would sweep up the jagged pieces of the broken teacup and move on, but he would die, again and again, for the rest of her life.

PRIDE AND BROOM

I T IS A WEDDING defined by what it is not.

There is no white dress. Dresses are not Parveen's style, and even if they were, she wouldn't be caught dead in a dress that supposedly stands for female virginity—which means, of course, being untouched by a *man*. She wouldn't be caught dead in anything designed to make her look like a porcelain doll. She is no porcelain doll.

There is no veil. Parveen isn't certain what the veil is supposed to represent, but she knows it has something to do with the notion that it is fitting and proper for a woman to reveal only part of herself. She doesn't see the difference between a wedding veil and a hijab, and she's been there and done that.

Something old? Aside from the trees in the park where the ceremony is being held, the oldest thing here is Parveen herself. She is forty-two, and ironically more aware of her age today, on her wedding day, than ever in her life.

Something new? Yes, her shoes are new, and they are killing her feet. She finds it appropriate somehow, that the "something new" that is supposed to represent the couple's fresh new life together is actually causing her pain.

Something borrowed? From whom is one supposed to borrow something, and what sort of thing is it supposed to be? If it is supposed to be a wedding dress borrowed from one's mother, Parveen's mother, as far as she knows, did not keep hers—and it wouldn't have fit Parveen anyway. And there's the minor detail that her mother is directly on the opposite side of the planet today.

Something blue? She assumes that this is supposed to be "baby blue," again representing feminine purity. She doesn't hate all shades of blue, but she detests that one. She could have worn blue jeans to this ceremony. It wouldn't have mattered. Maybe her underwear has some blue? She hasn't checked.

There is no bouquet thrown, no garter stripped from the thigh. Even if she wanted to wear a garter, she couldn't very well strip it from beneath the trousers of the suit she is wearing. She is holding a bouquet, a beautiful arrangement of wildflowers, but she will not throw it. She would not want someone she knows will never marry to catch it.

No bachelor or bachelorette party preceded this wedding, and there was no rehearsal dinner. What need was there to "rehearse" something that one did so naturally?

Nor does this wedding bear any similarity to those Parveen witnessed as a child in Iran. There is no sofre-ye-aghd, the magnificent floor spread with its seven herbs, seven pastries, and candelabras. There is no "mirror of fate" to reflect the beaming faces of the couple and set the tone for their future together. There is no sweetening of this union with ghand rubbed over a canopy, no frankincense sprinkled over hot coals to ward off evil. There could not have been a khastegaree or aghd, of course: there are no consenting families.

There is a marriage certificate, and thankfully, it is legal now in the United States. But it has no validity in Iran, where this union would be punishable by death. Even in the United States, there are still places where this certificate is not worth the paper it is written on or the cheap Walmart frame that surrounds it. Their marriage will still put targets on their backs.

There is a minister. She is a woman whose appointment caused a huge scandal in her congregation and prompted challenges from other members of the church. She wears a sparkling purple robe, and her knowledge of the gospel is vast, but some believe that she cannot possibly have genuine faith, cannot advocate the Christian life. This minister will sanctify the union, but only in some eyes.

And after it is over, there is no receiving line. There are no proud mothers standing tirelessly on foot in their immaculate dresses and coiffed hairstyles, beaming as they kiss guest after guest. There are no self-satisfied fathers grasping the hands or slapping the backs of those who have gathered to celebrate this milestone in their lives. Both mothers are absent: one because of physical distance and the other because of emotional distance. One father is a shadowy figure whose address no one knows, and the other father does not know of his daughter's marriage—must never learn of his daughter's marriage, for fear the knowledge will kill him.

But there are guests. They came in droves this morning, a veritable fleet of rainbow-stickered cars. They came in jeans and T-shirts, they came in suits and ties, they came in high heels and sandals, with makeup and without. They brought armloads of gifts, so many that the folding table could not hold them, and they spill over onto the grass.

"Here come the brooms!" the guests shout as the couple approaches. This is the title they have given themselves, the title they have used on their lighthearted wedding invitation. It is supposed to combine the words *bride* and *groom*, and they assume everyone will get it. It isn't exactly funny, but it does add some levity to the occasion. Even the minister has accepted this title. After the vows are over and she has sanctified the union, she looks from one to the other and says, smiling broadly and perhaps somewhat devilishly, "You may kiss the broom!"

Parveen steps forward in her spotless taupe-colored suit and her too-tight shoes. She looks at Maura, this woman with whom she will make a life; this woman who has promised her children by any means necessary; this woman with whom she has already selected semen that sits in the freezer in the home they already share. This woman she will never be able to love publicly in her own country, even though the love she feels for her is deeper and fiercer than any she has ever known.

Maura steps forward to meet her. Parveen looks at her strong, earnest face and sees that she is smiling, the dimples opening up in her cheeks like buttonholes. She looks beyond Maura at the lush green grass of the park, then up at the radiant summer sky. She knows this sky reaches all the way across the globe to Iran, but she feels at this moment that it is hers alone. She squeezes Maura's hand, then kisses her directly on the lips.

MARRIED LIFE, DAY 12,785

IT'S ONE OF THOSE MIDSUMMER AFTERNOONS IN GEORGIA that seems laden with significance, with light-streaked clouds bulging out against a screaming blue sky. I'm sitting in the grass reading, and Joaquín is working in the garden—*his* garden, he likes to call it. He is shirtless, and from where I sit in my lawn chair, I can see his weather-beaten back flashing through the stalks of corn and okra and his bony elbows jutting upward as he bends and straightens to prune and weed. He gardens with a kind of rapture, as though it were a sacred act. The attention he gives to plants and soil is the closest he comes lately to an expression of love.

Even though the day is waning, the sun is still beating down on me white-hot. Having grown up in the Middle East, I need the sunlight the way a lizard does, to energize me and stimulate my metabolism. I choose to ignore conventional wisdom about sun exposure and adhere instead to the subversive school of thought that believes it is actually the *lack* of sun that is dangerous. Today I have chosen to heed my mother's advice about wearing sunglasses, not because I agree with her that squinting in the sun will give me wrinkles, but because the tinted lenses make it easier to see the print on the pages of the book I am reading.

I have read *This Is How You Lose Her* before. I was in Boston when the book came out and went to hear Junot Díaz speak. The speech was mostly canned, which annoyed me, but I was strangely moved by the passage he read, and I stood in line to have my copy signed by the man himself. After the allegations surfaced, I was embarrassed to have been so starry-eyed, and I put the book away. I don't know why I am returning to it now, and why "Invierno" is resonating with me on a sweltering day in July.

I turn the book over and find myself staring into the somewhat unsettling face of the author, a large photo of whom appears on the back cover. Something Junot said during the Q&A is etched permanently in my mind, and I hear him snarling it again now as I stare at the sardonic smile that is his trademark. When a woman from the audience asked him why he found it necessary to use so many swear words in his books, he chortled derisively and said, "You know, here in the great US of A we do a lot of horrible things that we describe with lovely words, like dropping bombs on people and calling it 'spreading democracy.' So, yeah, I'm not going to bother defending myself for reproducing the way my people actually speak."

In the grass beneath my feet, a bee is hunched over on a clover flower, mustering all the energy in its tiny body for the task of coating its legs in pollen. Its movements are slight but precise, as if it were programmed to move exactly that way at exactly that angle at exactly that moment to absorb exactly that amount of pollen. If my information is correct, the bee will later carry this pollen elsewhere, and communicate the location of the pollen source to other bees through a waggle dance. With these seemingly insignificant gestures, this miniscule creature is touching off a butterfly effect that will change the whole universe.

I train my phone camera on the bee and zoom in so I can observe it more closely. It continues its work, unfazed by my violation of its privacy. At one point I imagine that it has eye contact with me, and that it's giving me the kind of smug, disinterested look my cat gives me when he knows I am admiring him. I consider doing a Google search about waggle dances, but this seems like an even greater violation of the bee's privacy. Besides, whatever I find there will be from the human perspective, with the added filter of the Heisenberg Uncertainty Principle. *And Schrödinger's cat could eat the bee*, I think to myself, then chuckle silently at my own lame joke, which could only come from a former philosophy student who has forgotten all but the basics of what she learned decades ago.

Looking back toward Joaquín in his garden, it occurs to me that he and I have a dance of our own. Where the bee's dance is mathematical and precise, ours is a study in random disorder. Even after three decades together, we still make the classic mistakes that novice dancers make: false starts, missed beats, toe-stepping, a general failure to get in sync. Over time we've added some deliberately oppositional jabs and feints. Most of the time we're not partners at all—we're combatants in a dance of defiance and conquest.

Part of the problem is that our medium is words. If we could just shut up a bit and use our bodies and our senses the way a bee does, we might move across the dance floor more effectively. The bee's dance is mystical and sublime, but words—at least ours—are insidious and manic. They're like electrical charges that continue to pulse through the air long after the signal was sent, zapping us when we least expect it.

Joaquín comes toward me now, a tomato cupped in his hands. From a distance he almost looks like an adolescent, with his lean legs and jaunty gait. It's only when he turns to the side that his hard, round belly—the product of decades of heavy drinking—becomes visible.

As he draws near, I can see the tomato he's carrying is oddly shaped, oversized, and purplish in color. It makes me think of cancer.

"Do you see this *cacho de tomate*?" Joaquín says. "Incredible, isn't it?"

Spanish is my third language; English is Joaquín's second—so naturally, Spanglish is our lingua franca. I know what a *cacho* is, and I know why Joaquín has chosen to use the Spanish word to describe his tomato. There simply is no English equivalent.

"*Es bonito*," I say. And the tomato is truly beautiful now that I am seeing it up close.

"*Es un* heirloom," he says, putting the accent on the second syllable the way you would in Spanish. "*Se llama* Cherokee Purple."

"Cool name," I say. Out of the corner of my eye I spot the bee lazily moving to another clover flower. I turn my head to watch it.

"*Qué miras?*"

If I tell Joaquín I'm watching a bee, he'll accuse me of being bored; of not knowing what to do with my time; of not being able to concentrate on my book; of just pretending to read. Even if he doesn't articulate these observations, I'll know he's thinking them. I could argue that gardening is his way of communing with nature and reflecting on the movements of a bee is mine—but we've had that conversation before, and it's not worth repeating.

"*Nada*," is all I say.

Still clutching his Cherokee Purple heirloom, Joaquín crosses the lawn, walks up the porch steps, and enters the house.

৩১

When I met Joaquín, he was pulsating with life, like a complex machine that was permanently switched on and constantly churned out meaning. I was fascinated by each cog and wheel, even more fascinated because I couldn't fully understand how the pieces fit together. I was just learning Spanish at the time, so I also couldn't grasp the fine details of what he was saying, especially when he held forth about politics or history, which he did often.

I met him on a street in Spain. The year was 1984, and I was just emerging from my own private Orwellian nightmare. I had finished my undergraduate degree in California a few years earlier, right at the time when Iran was in the throes of revolution. I decided to return and plunk myself down in the middle of what I thought would be a joyous period in my country's history: the transition to a true Marxist utopia. It wasn't long before I realized that what had been billed as progress was actually decline: my country was sliding backward toward the Middle Ages. Life in Khomeini's Iran was depressing. After the bombs started falling, it became intolerable.

As miserable as the Islamic Republic was, the prospect of returning to the States was even worse. I could be reasonably happy in the United States as long as I was inside the cocoon of academia—but the lofty discipline of philosophy that I had once found so stimulating now seemed like so much blah-blah-blah to me, and the thought of continuing my studies filled me with existential ennui. And so, armed with two suitcases and a prestigious but impractical degree, I boarded a plane to Madrid.

Life in post-fascist Madrid was as wild and raw as anything I had ever experienced. I found work at a language institute which paid enough for me to live in a well-equipped hostel with a shared kitchen in Chueca, a bustling neighborhood near the center of the city. I was determined to experience "the real Spain," so I stayed away from tourist traps and shunned the glitzy pub scene in favor of the dusty plazas where youths sat on the backs of park benches smoking canutos and bemoaning the state of the world. I fed my wine habit at the seamy bars I found in back alleys, side streets, and working-class barrios.

I had been living in Madrid for almost a year when I met Joaquín. There was a full moon that night; I remember this because I was trying to keep sight of it as I made my way up Calle Preciados, but the buildings and the neon lights kept getting in the way. I stopped for a minute in front of a department store and examined the window display. I remember feeling entranced by the mannequins and thinking that no one—not even Spanish women, who had more flair than any women I had ever met—actually dressed this way. My favorite costume at the time was a tight-fitting black top and loose-fitting black pants, sometimes accessorized with a necklace or a scarf. I was wearing that costume when I met Joaquín.

Lost in my thoughts in front of the window, I had the distinct sensation that someone was approaching me from behind. Spaniards were sometimes odd about their space, so I didn't turn around at first, not even after he spoke.

"*Voy a tomar algo alla en el bar de enfrente. ¿Te vienes?*"

The invitation was presumptuous, especially because it was delivered to my back. When I turned to look at him, he blinked at me—or maybe it was a wink. Then, without another word, he walked on in the direction of the bar.

I don't know what made me accept the invitation, but I did.

"*Espera,*" I said. "*Vamos.*"

Something about him reminded me of a puppet. He was all angles and joints, and his body bent in unexpected places. His legs were too long to sit comfortably on the barstool, so he swung them toward me until his left knee was touching my thigh. Through the fabric of my Kurdish trousers, his bones felt like wood. The sensation was oddly appealing. He was wearing a loose olive-green T-shirt, and beneath it I could make out the contours of his shoulder blades and his ribcage. I couldn't see his face well in the half-light of the bar, but it, too, looked like it had been chiseled out of wood. There were hollows and crevices where they didn't belong, as though whoever had carved him had used a blunt tool. His eyebrows rose and fell when he spoke, and his mouth swung open and snapped shut as though it were hinged together at the edges.

The first words he spoke were blunt. *"Tía, cuentame algo de tu vida."*

At the time it was in vogue for Spaniards, especially those who were in their twenties, to call each other tía and tío—aunt and uncle. The expression was part of the current youth argot, and it bugged me. But Joaquín used it naturally, and for the first time, I liked the way it sounded. But I didn't know where to begin to tell him about my life; how to explain why an Iranian woman with an American education was living in Madrid and walking through the streets alone. I struggled to present my story to him in my halting Spanish. It came out awkwardly, but he was quick.

"O sea, que eres una pija Irani-yanqui, y no tienes idea que hacer con tu vida." It hurt me that he immediately pegged me as a "spoiled brat Iranian-Yankee who has no clue what to do with her life." But I knew he was right.

და

The day after we met was the first time he called me pobrecita, and the way he said it made my blood run cold. It came completely out of nowhere. We were sitting on a bus on our way to El Escorial when he suddenly seized my hands, put them up to his cheeks, and said, *"Pobrecita. Tus manos están sudando. De que tienes miedo?"*

I didn't know exactly what the words meant, but I picked up on the subtext. I was twenty-four and determined to cultivate a strong woman image, so being called a *pobrecita*, a "poor child," was a shock. As for the other part, it was true: my hands *were* sweating, and I *was* afraid.

I realized what he was suggesting was that I was unnerved by his incisiveness, his intensity, his cleverness, and that was making my hands sweat. But that wasn't it at all. I was afraid of Joaquín, but what I was afraid of was a part of him I couldn't see; a part I knew he was keeping carefully hidden. I wanted to explain this to him, but when I opened my mouth to do so he leaned over and kissed me. The kiss seemed sincere, but after it was over, I noticed that the look on his face was blank, almost glassy-eyed. It was not a look that came from the healthy spinning of wheels and cogs—it was the sinister byproduct of a part of the machinery that was cold, a part whose job it was to keep the others in check.

I was completely bewitched by the machinery—far too bewitched to begin fashioning a shield. The sapio-sexual in me was turned on by the sharp edges of his mind, which provided a whetstone for my own. He wasn't American and he wasn't Iranian, which made everything about him feel exotic and new. I wanted him, body, mind, and soul.

∽

I stay outside until the sun begins to sink behind the tree line, then pick up my cell phone and my Junot Díaz and walk into the house.

Joaquín has cut up the heirloom tomato and is standing at the counter chopping some fresh basil leaves. He scoops the chopped leaves into his hands and sprinkles them over the tomato, then opens the refrigerator and pulls out the feta cheese.

"Are you hungry?" he asks without looking at me.

"Yeah," I say without looking at him.

We are mostly silent during dinner. Joaquín eats with his shirt off, and I try not to stare at his bulbous stomach and the loose skin on his neck. The few times we have eye contact, I avert my eyes from his yellowed teeth and the broken veins in his cheeks. His profile in my peripheral vision is vaguely crow-like. Age has hollowed his cheeks, accentuated his hooked nose, and fixed his thin lips in a permanent frown. I wonder which parts of my body he avoids looking at.

I compliment the tomato salad and the venison stew he has cooked. Both are, indeed, delicious. After the dishes are cleared, I sit down in my favorite reading chair and pick up *This Is How You Lose Her* again. Joaquín goes into the other room and turns on the television. On his way into the kitchen to pour his third glass of bourbon, he pauses in front of my armchair and stares down at the book cover. He is spoiling for a fight.

"How can you like that guy?" he asks in English. He flattens the vowel sound in the word *guy* so it sounds like *gay*, and I wonder if this is deliberate. "I thought he was a *mujeriego misógino*. At least that's what you liberal intellectuals say, right?"

I'm not sure which irks me more: that he has labeled Junot Díaz, whose books he has never read, a womanizing misogynist, or that he has labeled me a liberal intellectual. I know that both of these labels could change tomorrow: depending on his mood, Junot might be the voice of disenfranchised immigrants and I might be an ignoramus. I won't take the bait.

But Joaquín presses on. "To me he is just *un gilipollas vendido*," he says. This translates roughly as "a douchebag sellout."

"How do you know, if you've never read him?"

"I don't have to read that idiot to know what he's like. All I have to do is look at his face and I can tell he is one of those Latinos who capitalize on their heritage. It's easy to do that in this culturally impoverished country."

I spread the book open on my lap, print side up, so that the photograph won't be visible. Realizing that he's not going to get a rise out of me tonight, Joaquín fills his glass and heads back toward the television room. As he walks through the door, he delivers his parting line: "*Odio eterno al imperio Americano.*"

I know the reference well. The first time I heard it was the day Joaquín took me to meet his parents. His father, a good-natured Asturian who had worked all his life in a brick factory, had bathed and groomed himself for the occasion, and Joaquín teased him about his slicked-back hair and his pressed shirt. His mother, a squat woman with protruding breasts and a squeaky voice, had obviously dyed her graying hair that same day, but Joaquín made no mention of this. He was deferential around his mother, and I immediately detected the signs of a mama's boy. Even a working-class family could have a principito.

Alejandro and Teresa were both hard-core leftists, izquierdistas who had suffered greatly during Franco's años del hambre and had a deeply ingrained mistrust of all politicians. Both seemed pleased that their son, the first in the family to go to college, had found a girl-friend from the exotic and troubled Middle East. Being confirmed atheists, they couldn't possibly have approved of the Islamic Revolution, but their remarks about it were respectful and safe.

"At least Khomeini is better than that evil tyrant who used to run the country," Alejandro said.

"*A cada cerdo le llega su San Martin,*" Teresa said. "Every pig will eventually have his day of slaughter." I wasn't sure whether she was referring to Khomeini or to the Shah, but I nodded my head in agreement.

When the conversation turned to the United States, they were equally cautious, again treading lightly to avoid offending to me. I had no trouble following the conversation, and no trouble agreeing with the political views they expressed. But when Alejandro made a remark that caused his wife and son to burst into laughter, I was thoroughly confused.

"*¡Odio eterno al imperio Romano¡*"

I didn't get the joke. I understood the words, but the remark seemed like a non sequitur to me. We hadn't been talking about the Roman Empire, but about the American military bases in Torrejón and Rota. I asked Joaquín to explain.

"That's what Hannibal said during the Punic Wars when he swore an oath of eternal hatred toward Rome. My father is drawing a parallel between the United States and the Roman Empire. What he means is that he hates the *American* Empire. He's just too polite to say so directly."

I looked at Alejandro and smiled. "*Estoy completamente de acuerdo*," I said. And I did completely agree.

Lying in our bed in the hostel later that night, I found myself waxing nostalgic about life in the United States. I told Joaquín about the foothills near Palo Alto, about Big Sur, about the cable cars in San Francisco, about the Golden Gate Bridge. He listened and nodded, and for once he didn't have any biting comments to offer. At one point when I paused my narrative to take a sip of wine, he propped himself up on his elbows and said, without a touch of irony in his voice, "*Tía*, why don't we move to Estados Unidos? Maybe I should see up close what I have been fighting against all these years, like Don Quixote fighting windmills."

"Let's do it," I said.

A few months later we landed in El Imperio Americano.

❧

Joaquín has retreated to the other room; I can hear him plopping his body down heavily onto the couch. He has left the door open so that the television shoots bolts of blue and green light into the hallway. At intervals his laughter rises above the muffled sounds of a Spanish comedy show. I know he's laughing as loud as he can just to piss me off.

It's working. I can't concentrate on reading. I flip the book closed and am confronted again with Junot Díaz's self-satisfied mug. I know Joaquín has a point: the guy is probably a slimeball. But Junot Díaz isn't Joaquín's target—I am.

I have a sudden urge to fight back; to go into the television room and shout at him. The words hijo de puta well up in my throat. I have near-native command of Spanish now, and I can deliver the insult with a guttural jota sound that will give it maximum effect. But hijo de puta is *his* expression, in *his* language. Besides, I don't want to utter the word puta; don't even want it to exist in my vocabulary. And his mother might have been a bitch sometimes, but she wasn't a whore.

Pedar-sag, I think to myself. Pedar-sag.

Joaquín has heard this insult many times before, and knows it means "your father is a dog." If I were to say this to him now, it might enrage him, but it would fail to have the desired impact. He would counter by saying that his father was *not* a dog, which is certainly true. Alejandro was a gentle, almost saintly man who spoke little and always softly. He could sit for hours looking out over the tiny plot of land he owned in the mountains of Avila, barely moving a muscle, perfectly at peace. He was the antithesis of the kind of dog the expression pedar-sag conjured up.

There's a reason why the word machismo originated in Spain, why it is borrowed into other languages wholesale instead of being translated. All those disgusting swaggering males dating back to the ancient Iberians; you would think they would have updated by now. But Joaquín's father wasn't like that.

What Joaquín will never get is that pedar-sag has nothing to do with fathers. It's not the reference to fathers that is an insult—father insults are far less visceral and hurtful than mother insults in Iranian culture. It's the dog part that makes pedar-sag so denigrating.

Joaquín can't possibly understand the weight of a dog insult in Farsi. He knows that dogs are considered dirty in Islam, but he has never experienced this firsthand.

I grew up seeing dogs abused, chained up, and fed nothing but dry crusts of bread, their ears and tails lopped off to make them mean. Joaquín grew up in a culture where it was a sign of prosperity to have a dog. He laughs at the way I tend to our dogs, calls it "bourgeois" to care so much about domestic animals when there are suffering people in the world. Being from a working-class family, he believes he has an authentic connection to dogs—he understands their rank in the unjust hierarchy of the universe.

I know, of course, that this is bullshit. Like with his garden, what Joaquín loves about dogs is the control he can exercise over them. He waits until they are begging before he feeds them, derives pleasure from watching them salivate in anticipation of his generosity. If a dog is sick, he will patently refuse to treat it. If it dies, it's just "*la ley de la vida*"—the law of life.

Maybe that's why, when he found our dog writhing in pain on the couch one morning, he took her outside and shot her with his hunting rifle.

I wasn't there when it happened, but he told me what he had done with no discernible emotion, as though it were just an ordinary part of his day. I was too horrified to be angry at first; I spent a few days in stunned silence. When I was finally able to speak about what he had done, I pointed out that mistreating animals was a classic trait of abusive people.

True to form, Joaquín scoffed at my reaction, calling it childish and misguided. "What did you expect me to do, send the dog to college?" he laughed.

My use of the term "abusive" was just "American pop psychology." Putting a dog out of its misery was not abusive, he insisted.

The thousands of dollars the vet would have charged him—*that* was abusive.

The incident happened several years ago, and I am mostly over it now. But I think about it again as the words pedar-sag reverberate through my brain, and I contemplate going into the room where he is watching a comedy show and throwing it up in his face again.

Or I could march into the television room and ask him why, if he hates the American Empire so much, he is still living here. But I could ask myself that too.

∾

Six days ago was our thirty-fifth wedding anniversary, an event that we did not celebrate and never have celebrated. I have always had a thing for numerology, so I pull out my phone and put in the numbers. According to Planetcalc, we have been married for 12,785 days. 420 months. 306,600 hours, give or take. We were married in the twentieth century, and it is now the twenty-first. No matter how I add and subtract the digits in the effort to find meaning, nothing comes.

We had planned to get married on the Fourth of July—it would be our own private joke, the satirical relevance of which no one but us would understand. City Hall was closed on the Fourth, of course, so we chose the next day instead. The details of our marriage are not glamorous. The decision to get married was a practical one: Joaquín's visa was running out. We took public transportation to the courthouse, stopping on the way to do the required blood tests. No family members were present, so we pulled a woman we didn't know off the street to act as a witness. After we signed on the dotted line, we went straight to the welfare office and got food stamps. I was wearing a red sweater and jeans. No photographs were taken.

I think back on the many Fourth of Julys we have spent in this country. There was the time we went to Stone Mountain to see the fireworks and our daughter had a near panic attack, holding her hands over her ears and screaming, "No bangs! No bangs!" There was the time Joaquín's niece was visiting from Spain and we took her to Home Depot, where we ate hot dogs and then sat in a tiny strip of grass outside the store and watched the fireworks on the other side of the parking lot. There was the year we bought our son some bottle rockets made in China with the hilarious label that read "Stick butt end in ground. Light fuse. Run away."

Every year, no matter where we have been, Joaquín has felt the need to remind me that fireworks in the United States can never compare to those in Spain. Spaniards are true fire-worshippers, he says. They love to court danger, which is why they love bullfights. They all carry Unamuno's existentialism, his *sentimiento trágico de la vida*, in their DNA. Americans just want an excuse to eat greasy food, get drunk, and fan the fires of patriotism.

A week ago, we sat on the porch after dinner. It was a rainy night, and neither of us remembered it was the Fourth of July. Rain and pandemic notwithstanding, Woodstock, Georgia, was determined to celebrate. The explosions were mostly hidden from view, but the sounds were loud enough to frighten the dogs. The brave one, our mutt, lifted his head and howled as though he might scare the fireworks away. The cowardly one, our Australian shepherd, slunk inside and hid under the bed. Joaquín and I just sat there on the porch, he with his bourbon and me with my cabernet, listening, without reacting, to the booming and crackling and whizzing that accompanied the distant flashes of light in the sky.

What is there to celebrate about our lives here? What has the United States given us? Social Security numbers that might be used to gather information about us. Retirement benefits, as long as they don't dry up. A home we like to think is ours, but that will belong to the bank for at least another decade. What have we given back? Lots of money in taxes that go to things we don't approve of. The inevitable excursions to Target and Walmart and Home Depot to buy things we don't need. More recently, purchases that line the pockets of Jeff Bezos and others like him. Years of enriching tobacco companies and alcohol manufacturers.

When we moved to the United States, we were convinced that living in a neutral country would be a great equalizer for us. We would share an income bracket, which would erase the class differences from our past. Our native cultures would be ignored or maligned equally, and we would be united in the effort to keep them alive. We would band together against our common enemy: American myopia and ignorance. Instead, after almost three decades here, the American Empire seems to have heightened our incompatibility. Life in the American Empire has crystallized in us the worst parts of the cultures we left behind. His machismo. My defensiveness. His need to rank-order everything in the universe and come out on top. My impulse to lash out when I am hurt. His cynicism. My secrecy.

Maybe it's because we're fighting for the same leftover piece of pie—the piece that has hardened on the plate and that no one wants. We are each desperate for our words, our accents, our sensibilities to rise to the top in this monolithic, monolingual place we have grudgingly chosen to call home.

I guess we have somehow melted into the proverbial pot. It has annihilated our original flavors, but we can still taste traces of them. Joaquín is the bay leaf—the ingredient that is essential to the recipe but that you can't actually eat. I'm the turmeric—the miracle root that is suddenly everywhere and now seems to have been discovered right here on American soil, even though it's part of the ancient cuisine I have been eating all my life. Bay leaves and turmeric don't belong in the same stew, but here we are.

Life in America has brought all of this out: the stark differences between us, our basic incompatibility, the ways we have grown to dislike each other, the parts of ourselves we guard jealously and don't let the other touch, our complacency about the whole concept of marriage.

At the same time, life in America has joined us, maybe not at the hip, but with some kind of invisible thread that unites us precisely because we live here. Our status as outsiders has forced us to go through the rungs of hell, and the process has somehow brought us full circle, back to that street in Chueca where we found each other when we were both wandering like lost souls. We pretend to love neither America nor one another—but the truth is that somehow, we have ended up with a tangled kind of love that includes both. We wouldn't still be together otherwise, and we wouldn't still be here.

I think I remember reading that honeybees didn't exist on the American continent until they were brought here from Europe by the colonists. I wonder: did their waggle dance change after they got to the American Empire, or did it retain its original European character?

I'm not going to Google it. I'm just going to sit here in my armchair until it's time to go to bed.

RAGHEAD

S HE WOULDN'T HAVE KNOWN HIM ANYWHERE. It is a reversal of
the idiom, she knows, but the thing is, she *should* have known
him anywhere. She has been carrying him around for decades
now, connected to him as if by an umbilical cord.

The face that looks back at her from the Facebook page has no
resemblance to the face of that wiry kid who was responsible for what
she has come to see as a seminal moment in her life. Although the
precise details of the day have been mostly buried and the contours
of the memory are blurry, the event itself has never disappeared from
her psyche. Yes, she thinks now as she looks at the photograph, *psyche*
is the appropriate word for the place she keeps the memory of Dave
Abbott. In mythology, Psyche was a goddess who stole worshipers
from Venus and was punished when Cupid shot an arrow at her to
make her fall in love with the first hideous thing she saw. Instead, she
ended up confined to a bedroom where she was visited nightly by an
unidentified lover. Dave Abbott isn't hideous, and he certainly isn't a
secret lover, but Arya can feel an arrow piercing some part of her as
she looks at his image on the screen.

The most intense experience of her life belonged to Dave Abbott.
It was a clear line of demarcation in her timeline, dividing her reality
into before and after. She has told the story of Dave Abbott to her

children, to her students, to her friends, even to strangers at a party. Each time she recounts the incident, she embellishes it differently depending on her mood and her audience. Sometimes the story is gruesome, sometimes it is tender, sometimes it is just a humorous anecdote. But always, no matter when, how, or to whom she has told the Dave Abbott story, she has told it with a certain lightheartedness, as though it were nothing to her. Telling it this way is a form of self-protection. It has allowed her to hide, even from herself, the mixture of guilt and shame the memory provokes. Guilt and shame and some other emotion she has never been able to identify.

Arya likes to claim she isn't much of a Facebooker, but this isn't exactly true. Going on Facebook clashes with her political ideals and with her personality, and it isn't unusual for people who find her on the site to remark, "You're the last person I expected to find on Facebook!" Her first hesitant posts were political in nature: reposted memes about refugees, articles from *The Guardian* or *The Nation*, an occasional opinion piece of her own. Even when these posts garnered "likes," they seemed utterly meaningless when juxtaposed with photos of friends frolicking on a beach or posts announcing every ingredient of someone's dinner. She began, instead, to scroll through her feed quickly, wish people a happy birthday, and shut the platform down.

It was a series of clicks that led Arya to Dave Abbott. A former classmate she had known at the Shemiran American School posted an article about an art show featuring contemporary Iranian painters. She opened it and skimmed it. In the comments section beneath the article, she noticed the name of Jennifer Abbott, Dave's older sister. She clicked on Jennifer's name and found, among her "friends," the name David Abbott. Seeing that name stopped her heart, but she clicked.

In his profile photo he is wearing a hat, for which she is thankful. She doesn't want to see what she suspects to be thinning hair, possibly even a bald head, replacing what used to be soft golden curls. The hat is Indiana Jones, which doesn't seem to fit with the nine-year-old kid she remembers, a kid who was always doodling, drawing sardonic cartoons on the corners of his homework. The kid who once gave her a chewed nub when she asked to borrow a pencil.

But there is something in the eyes that sparks recognition. The same half-stare, half-smirk, as though he is looking directly into her soul and right through her at the same time. The same bright eyes that come partly from genetics, but mostly from a glittering intellect. The same expression he had worn that fateful day: an expression that defied her to come and get him. There is an air of mystery about him, mixed with an air of cynicism. It's as if Ambrose Bierce has come back a century after his disappearance in Mexico and is alive and well.

He is not a handsome man, and he had not been a handsome child. And yet her heart pounds as she looked into the eyes of the photograph and feels them looking back. She begins to scroll through his page, pretending to herself that she doesn't care what she finds there. There isn't much that bothers her or surprises her. There are lots of cartoons drawn by Dave Abbott himself, very good ones, mostly relating to topical issues like the environment, the addiction to cell phones, the excessive military budget. There are many pictures of dogs. There is a series of photographs of guys sitting in front of a fire with cans of beer in their hands. There are photographs of Dave Abbott on a stage, presumably in a play. There is a photograph of him at a gallery with a glass of wine in his hand.

Arya scrolls through his posts and finds several long anti-Trump rants. She doesn't read these closely—she has heard it all before—but she is relieved. There are several other lengthy posts, many of them about the art scene. She pauses to read a recent one about how much he hates the *putti* in Italian paintings. He writes well.

There isn't much in his *About* section. If he ever graduated from college, he's not saying so. It seems he was once married and divorced, but he appears to have no children. *Work and Education* have been left blank. *The Life Events* section has been left blank. *Relationship Status* is identified as "Single," and next to *Interested In*, he has written "Women." He is no longer Dave Abbott, but now goes by David. He lives in Bisbee, Arizona. He has 227 friends.

There is not one word about his childhood in Iran.

⋘⋙

Arya hasn't thought about the Shemiran American School in a while, but she has researched the school's history as an adult. The school was seized during the Islamic Revolution, shortly after Arya and her family fled the country and settled in the United States, but its origins went back more than a century. It had been started by a group of missionaries in the late nineteenth century and had been expanded in the years following President Truman's Point Four Program, which brought a flood of Americans into Iran.

Even though she last saw it more than forty years ago, she can still picture the campus. There were several buildings on the compound, the main one a large, quaint brick building that had once been a hospital. The hallways inside were painted pale green like the hallways of an American public school. A football field stretched out to one side of the campus, its lush grass sneering at the rubble and dust that surrounded it. The whole compound was enclosed by a tall brick wall with barbed wire on top, reminiscent of a prison camp. From the rooftop of the main building, the stars and stripes flapped in the wind.

Technically, only those with American passports were allowed to attend SAS. Among its most famous alumnae were Bob Barr, who later became a successful politician, and Norman Schwarzkopf, who went on to earn a Purple Heart for his bravery in Vietnam. The American students fell into three categories: they were from military families, oil company families, or missionary families. The school did allow a select few Iranian students. Arya was never sure how these students were chosen, but they all had one thing in common: they were filthy rich. Arya did not fit into any of these categories. She was allowed to attend the school only because her mother was a math teacher there.

The Iranian students gained a lot of social mileage from throwing their money around, but their wealth could not buy them something that every student at the school coveted: commissary privileges. The commissary was a store inside the US Embassy compound that was open only to American citizens. The products sold there were passed from hand to hand in the school like precious gems: Cheetos, Snickers bars, dainty bottles of Jergens lotion that smelled like cherries. Of all the commissary's treasures, Bazooka Joe bubblegum with waxy comic strips inside was the most precious. The American students who chewed it were always blowing huge bubbles, a behavior Arya found very impolite. They were the same students whose scalps were visible beneath their crew cuts and whose blue eyes seemed to shoot lasers at her. They seemed to exist on a higher plane, and she was frightened of them.

Although Dave Abbott did chew Bazooka Joe bubblegum, he hadn't really been like those other gum-smacking kids. She had been frightened of him too, but for very different reasons. Somewhere inside her fourth-grade brain, she had an inkling he might be a genius. She was both drawn to him and repulsed by him. Until the incident that changed everything.

❧

She shuts down the computer and walks over to her bookshelf. She has a collection of yearbooks from her SAS days, and she knows exactly which one she will find Dave Abbott in: 1973. She realizes, as she opens to book to Mrs. Hallford's fourth-grade class picture, that she doesn't remember much about the other students. She is not surprised to find that there are no students of color. One of the students is somewhat swarthy and looks like he might be Filipino, but she can't remember his name. She immediately identifies Shohreh Firouz, a half-Iranian girl who inherited some of her father's Middle Eastern features. Everybody else is in the photo is decidedly American: tall, robust, and blond. Arya, standing on the front row, is dwarfed by them, and her olive skin is immediately noticeable.

Standing right next to her in the front row is Dave Abbott. He is tiny, snaggle-toothed, and mean-looking, with patches of piebald skin and hair so blond it is almost white. He is standing stiffly in the photo, but looking at his picture gives Arya a strong memory of the way he moved his nine-year-old body: the loping gait that was part rebellion, part defeat; the awkwardly flailing limbs and bony elbows.

She stares at the image of Mrs. Hallford, who she realizes is now surely dead. Mrs. Hallford, the spinster missionary who had been in Iran for ten years and whose Farsi did not extend beyond "Salaam-Alaikum." Mrs. Hallford, who used to groom herself in class, standing in the light of the window with a handheld mirror, plucking her eyebrows and the hairs from her chin. Mrs. Hallford, who kept three pairs of shoes under her desk: high heels for her arrival, flat-heeled, practical shoes for the classroom, and sneakers for playground duty. Mrs. Hallford, who offered her used clothing, including her bras and panties, for sale at school. Mrs. Hallford, who did not offer Arya any support when the incident happened, and barely looked at her for the rest of the year after it did.

❧

It is inevitable: she must relive it. She must go back in time and walk around inside that day; bring her nine-year-old self back to life and inhabit her, body and mind.

Closing her eyes, she feels the pencil between her fingers as she writes the last word of her spelling test. She sees the paper cut lengthwise with the tidy row of her answers running down one side. She hears the click of her pencil case as she closes it to prepare for recess. She sees the witchy figure of Mrs. Hallford moving down the row and reaching out to collect her test.

And there he is: Dave Abbott. He is sitting one row back, not directly behind her but at just the right angle for her to catch him in her peripheral vision—not to see him, but to be aware of his furtive movements, his mouth-breathing, his thin lips emitting an occasional snarling noise. She gets out of her seat when her row is called to line up for recess, and suddenly he is right there behind her. He pokes her back with what feels like a piece of sharp metal but is probably just his spindly finger. "Hey donkeyhead," he says, "Wanna play with me today?"

She heads for the swing set as quickly as she can, hoping Dave Abbott will not catch up with her. She climbs onto the last remaining swing, thankful that Dave Abbott will not be able to swing beside her. But he does not give up: he finds a spot in the sand and begins to toss pebbles at her legs. He times it strategically so that the pebbles hit her legs each time the swing comes back down to the center of its arc, and they sting. There is a demonic grin on his face.

She can feel the dull breeze lifting the playground dust around her legs as the swing hits its low point; she can see the screaming blue sky overhead dotted by a few stratus clouds; she can see the chipped paint on the poles of the swing set. It is shocking how vividly the scene is playing in her mind now—so vividly that she can hear details of the exchange between herself and Dave Abbott that she had not remembered.

"I said I didn't want to play with you! Why can't you leave me alone?"

"I *am* leaving you alone, donkeyhead! I'm just playing with these pebbles, see?"

"I'm going to tell Mrs. Hallford if you don't stop bothering me."

"Awww, gonna go crying to the teacher? Okay, I'll leave you alone. But could I just have one little ride first?"

Here Arya pauses to consider the sexual implications of this statement, but she quickly dismisses the idea as absurd. This was a nine-year-old child—a child who probably still sucked his thumb when no one was looking. It was unlikely he knew that the reference to "riding" carried any innuendo. But what about the name he was calling her? Was "donkeyhead" a reference to her Iranian heritage—to the donkeys that roamed the streets of Tehran and served as transport vehicles for the many residents who could not afford a car?

And now, here it comes: the moment that changed everything. It plays in her mind like a movie in slow motion. She jumps off the swing, her yellow dress billowing around her as she descends. She bends down and picks up a sharp-edged rock that is lying in the sand. She looks straight into the eye of Dave Abbott, her tormentor, and hurls the rock in his direction. She hears the dull thud of the rock as it strikes Dave Abbott's head. She sees the way his head thrusts back as the rock hits him. She pictures his tiny body lying on the ground and the blood seeping through his blond hair and staining the sand. She envisions the rock itself lying inert beside Dave Abbott's crumpled body. It is a scene from an American war movie.

The inquisition that followed in Principal Whitlock's office plays in her mind with the clarity of a book on tape.

"Arya, did you throw this rock at David?"

"He was calling me names. He was throwing pebbles at me. He always bothers me. Every single day."

"But did you throw a rock at him?"

"I don't remember. I didn't mean to hit him."

But Arya *had* meant to hit him. It's as clear as day to her now. She had thrown the rock in a moment of anger, but she had taken aim. She had wanted to see Dave Abbott's blood spilling out of his tiny, annoying head. She had wanted to hurt him because he was shorter than her and not as smart as her and not as nice as her, and yet he had power over her. He had the power of the playground bully; the power of the short kid who develops a compensatory meanness; the power a nine-year-old boy has over a nine-year-old girl. Most of all, he had the power that came with his blondness: the ability to throw pebbles at her, to tease her, to harass her, to call her names. He had the power that came with being the son of an American military officer stationed in Iran but living in little America.

She remembers how her cheeks burned when she entered the classroom the next day and felt the eyes of all her blond, freckled classmates upon her. She remembers how she was shunned, even ridiculed openly by them, for the rest of the year. She remembers Dave Abbott coming to school three days later with his head bandaged, making jokes about being a mummy. She remembers him telling his classmates, gleefully, that the gash was four inches long and required eleven stitches. She remembers that the injury gave Dave Abbott the status of a hero, while she curled into a ball and barely made eye contact with anyone for months.

❧

She has finally done it—she has dug this memory up, gone back there, relived it, and can now file it away again. But suddenly, unbidden and unwelcome, another memory comes flooding into her consciousness. It is a memory she has buried even deeper than the memory of hitting Dave Abbott with a rock.

The year before the Dave Abbott incident, Arya's first year at SAS, she and her mother were walking into the schoolyard one morning when they saw a group of high school boys gathered on the street in front of the school. As they got closer, they noticed that the boys had formed a circle around some construction workers who were taking a break to have their morning tea. The boys, whose white skin and barrel-shaped chests contrasted with the lean, dark figures of the squatting workmen, were laughing loudly and pointing toward the men. Arya's mother grasped her hand tightly, and the two of them stopped walking. They were several meters away from the boys, but they could hear what they were saying.

"Hey, look!" one of them said, in a voice that was both gleeful and aggressive. "It's the ragheads!"

Arya had heard the term "raghead" before and knew it was a reference to the rags that Iranian workmen wore on their heads to protect them from the sun. She remembers feeling comforted by the realization that the workers spoke only Farsi and therefore couldn't understand what the boys were saying. In fact, they pretended like they couldn't hear them at all, and blithely continued drinking their tea.

But the boys weren't going to let it go. "Hey raghead," one of them said, "what do you have for lunch in that pail? Sheep guts or something?"

"It's probably sheep dung," another boy chimed in.

"Yeah, smells like it," the other boy said. "Or maybe that's the smell of not bathing for three days."

The workmen continued to ignore the boys. But then, out of nowhere, one of the boys picked up a rock and flung it toward the construction site. It landed squarely on the back of one of the workmen. All of the men scattered.

"Hey, hey!" the boys shrieked. "Look at those cowards go! They're too lazy to work, but they can sure run when they're scared!"

Arya's mother yanked her hand, moved her past the boys, and pulled her through the gates of the school. The boys erupted into laughter at the sight of the dark-haired math teacher and her dark-haired daughter slinking in. They knew Arya's mother had been watching them from a distance, but no one at the school would believe her word over theirs.

Arya and her mother had made it to the auditorium just in time for the assembly. After they said the Pledge of Allegiance with their hands over their hearts, Principal Whitlock gave the students their daily reminder that all they had to do was to look around them to see how fortunate they were and to realize that others didn't have the same privileges they had. He closed the assembly, as always, with the words "God Bless America."

✍

Arya closes the yearbook, lays her head back against the couch, and closes her eyes. She is no longer seeing memories or hearing voices. She is thinking.

What, exactly, has she felt toward Dave Abbott throughout these five decades? Her feelings have had the intensity of hate, but it hasn't been hate she has harbored: it has been obsession. She has been obsessed with him the way a murderer is obsessed with his victim, the way a hunter is obsessed with his prey. At the age of nine she wanted to hit him, but it wasn't exactly physical pain she had wanted to inflict. She had wanted to find his vulnerabilities and use them to dominate him. She had wanted to shrink him down to size, to put him in her pocket and carry him around so he could see the world through her eyes. She had wanted him to grovel, to writhe, to be humbled, to have some respect.

And now, at the age of sixty, she wants all of that again.

GHABELEH HAMLEH *

THE POUNDING IN AMENEH'S TEMPLES WON'T LET UP, and it's beginning to scare her. She has had headaches before, but this is different—it feels like something foreign has invaded her body and is occupying every square inch of it, from the tips of her fingers, which won't stop tingling, to the pit of her stomach, which feels like it is being twisted and kneaded like bread dough.

Maybe if she takes a walk, the pounding and tingling will subside. Ever since she arrived in the camp, she has been longing to go out to the far edge of it, the part that hangs over the water. If she keeps her head down, she can avoid eye contact with the other refugees who cross her path. She is not ready to communicate with anyone yet.

It is only Ameneh's third day at the camp. So far she has been lucky enough to sleep in a tent by herself, even though the camp is overcrowded and she has seen whole families sleeping on the bare ground wrapped in nothing but blankets. The Farsi interpreter at the

---

* At last count in 2023, there were an estimated 35,000 Afghan refugees in Greece. Many of these refugees arrive in Greece in boats from Turkey, often facing a treacherous journey across the Aegean Sea. Some Afghan refugees originated in Iran, which is home to approximately 3 million Afghans. Afghans are a marginalized community in Iran, and there are frequent deportations of undocumented Afghans as well as widespread reports of human rights abuses of Afghans by Iranian authorities, including public executions.

registry, an older Iranian woman, told Ameneh she would be given a single tent for a few days until they could find a family for her to lodge with. This, the woman told her, was because Ameneh was ghabeleh-hamleh—open to attack. At first Ameneh was insulted—to call her ghabeleh-hamleh was to suggest that she was weak. But the interpreter went on to explain, "It's because you're a young, single woman, and you are here alone." She lowered her voice and added, "It's better for you if they label you this way. You will have more comfortable accommodations, and they might process your paperwork faster."

When Ameneh steps out of her tent, the sky is overcast and there is a strong wind. She passes through row after row of tents, crosses the empty lot at the center of the camp, and reaches the promontory—the only side of the camp that is not enclosed by chicken wire. The wind whips at her headscarf and billows her skirt, but the cold air feels good against her face. She sits with her back against a boulder and squints across the water at the distant shoreline. This, she knows, is Turkey, where she boarded an overcrowded raft just a few days ago and made the terrifying journey across the sea. Whenever she has thought back on this journey, she has been unable to stop reliving one moment of it: the moment when a dark object fell out of the raft and sank beneath the surface of the water. She closed her eyes and ears at the time and convinced herself that it was a backpack that had fallen. She convinces herself again now.

In her peripheral vision, Ameneh can see another figure sitting on a boulder to her left. The words ghabeleh-hamleh leap into her mind. There is no one here but the two of them, and she is, indeed, open to attack. But when she musters her courage and turns to look at the figure, she realizes it is a child. She recognizes him: she has seen the boy repeatedly over the past three days. Every time she has seen him, he has been alone, and Ameneh knows this means he has made the journey to the camp without his family. He can't be more than nine or ten years old.

The boy's face is turned away from her, but she pictures his beautiful, unmistakably Afghan features in her mind's eye: the mop of dark hair, the slanted eyes rimmed with long lashes, the high cheekbones. He is wearing rubber slippers that are several sizes too big for him and a jacket that is too small. His gaze is fixed on the sea. Ameneh pictures him standing on the shores of Turkey alone and terrified, being squeezed into a vessel carrying three times the number of people it is designed to carry, not having anyone to comfort him when the dinghy pitches and tosses in the choppy water.

Her impulse is to go over and talk to the child, but she decides against it. She doesn't want to frighten him. She will return to the camp and leave him alone with his thoughts. As she passes by him, she whispers, "Salaam Alaikum." The boy doesn't answer, but he turns to her and there is a moment of understanding—perhaps even a faint smile.

When she gets back to the camp, she realizes she has missed lunch. It is a mistake to skip a meal in the camp, because there will be no food available until the next one. Hunger will only increase the pounding in her temples and the prickling sensations which have now extended to her toes, but it is a relief not to have to stand in the food line. There are always large groups of Syrians in the line, and they make Ameneh uncomfortable. They greatly outnumber the other refugees at the camp, and this gives them too much power. The African refugees scare her, with their dark, lean bodies, their shifty eyes, and their furtive movements. The Pakistanis are secretive. The Kurds are proud.

As for the Afghans, they have mostly ignored her so far. Ameneh knows that rumors about her are circulating. She is not one of them. Her parents are Afghans, but Ameneh herself has never been to Afghanistan. She was born and raised in Iran, in a small hut at the edge of a large estate where her parents worked for a wealthy Iranian couple as gardener and maid. The language she speaks most comfortably is Farsi, not Dari. She thinks of herself as Iranian.

Her parents do not know she is here. No one knows she is here. Several months ago, she fled the abusive man her parents forced her to marry and somehow found her way to Turkey, and from there to this camp in Lesvos.

Ameneh must find a way to deal with the beast inside her, which has now taken hold of her lungs, making it difficult for her to breathe. There is a dull ache in her chest, and her throat feels as though it is about to close up. Maybe some cold water on her face will help. This means, of course, that she has to go to the latrine.

Ameneh has learned to shut down parts of her olfactory apparatus since she has been in this camp. Otherwise she would not be able to tolerate the fetid smell that hangs permanently in the air. She has seen men in bright yellow vests sweeping certain areas of the camp and has noticed how lazily and inefficiently they do it, collecting only the largest pieces of garbage and pushing the smaller pieces further and further into the corners until they are impossible to retrieve and left there to rot. The latrine is cleaned every day with a hose, but she has traced the path of the swill that runs out from beneath it and has noticed that it has nowhere to go; it gathers in puddles and the dirt eventually absorbs it.

Just outside the entrance to the latrine, she feels suddenly light-headed. She tries to steady herself, but her legs give way beneath her, and she falls to the ground. When she comes to, an aid worker is bending over her, her face so close that Ameneh can see her pores. She feels hands beneath each of her armpits, hoisting her to her feet. She glances down and sees her headscarf lying in the dirt. The aid worker stoops to retrieve the scarf and places it in Ameneh's hands.

The women steer her toward the clinic. She feels her legs beginning to buckle again, but as soon as she is inside the doctor approaches her and eases her into a chair. He is an older man, perhaps the age of her father, and his round belly is visible beneath his white uniform. She has never been touched by a male who wasn't a family member, but she does not resist when he puts his fingers against her face and pulls back her eyelids, when he lifts her headscarf and moves his fingers up and down her neck, even when he pushes back the neckline of her shirt and places a cold metal gadget against her chest, right above the curve of her breast. She complies when he asks her to pull up her sleeve and helps him to slide the cuff around the bare flesh of her upper arm.

A look of alarm crosses the doctor's face when he studies the number on the dial. He turns toward Ameneh and addresses her directly even though he knows she can't understand the words he is speaking. The interpreter translates: "You are too young to have such high blood pressure. You are having a panic attack."

The doctor disappears into the back room of the clinic and returns with two small white pills in his hand. The nurse fills a plastic cup with water and tells Ameneh to take the pills. "These are tranquilizers," she says. "They will help you to relax, which is what you need most right now. Tonight you must sleep, and tomorrow you must come back to check your blood pressure again."

Dark clouds are gathering in the sky by the time Ameneh leaves the clinic. She is far too drowsy to wait in the line for the evening meal. She walks slowly back to her tent, falls onto her pallet, pulls the blanket around her, and sleeps.

She is awakened a few hours later by the sound of explosions in the sky. Her first thought is that the camp is under attack. She waits for the next explosion to come, and when it does, she is relieved—almost amused—by her mistake. Sharp flashes of lightning are now visible through the canvas of the tent, and the wind is so fierce that the structure is threatening to collapse. The rain has begun to seep through the seams, soaking the ground beneath her pallet. She cocoons herself inside her blanket and tries to tune out the sounds. Before long, she drifts to sleep again.

The next time she awakens, it is to a sound of rustling inside her tent. Some kind of creature—maybe a rat—has found its way inside. Whatever the creature is, she decides it will not harm her; it is just seeking shelter from the storm that is still raging outside. But when she feels it pawing at her blanket, she stiffens. Just as she is lifting her arms to bat the creature away, there is a sensation of warm breath against her cheek, followed by the sound of panting. Human breath and human panting.

Ghabeleh-hamleh. The words echo in her mind. But then, a flash of lightning illuminates the face of her invader, revealing his high cheekbones, his slanted eyes, and his mop of hair. She raises the edge of the blanket to make room for the boy, then hugs his body to hers and strokes his tear-drenched face with her fingertips.

ZENDEGI

THE FIRST TIME THE shouting began in the streets, you had the sensation that it was coming from right outside your bedroom window. This was just your imagination, of course. Even if the mobs had wanted to come to the northern part of Tehran where you lived with your parents, they would not have had the means to get there, nor would their voices have been able to penetrate the high garden walls and thick glass windows of your home. The residents of this part of the city—those who had not fled to Europe or the United States—had managed to remain immune to the shouting. They had taken to shuttering their windows and staying inside, where they huddled around their television sets and watched the action on the screen, even though it was happening just a few miles away.

You were seventeen years old when the shouting began. In some part of your being you had never recognized, let alone expressed, you knew it was justified—and you knew, though it frightened you, that people like your parents were the target of the shouters' wrath. The Shah's desperate gestures—releasing political prisoners, replacing his corrupt prime minister with a more likable one, claiming that he "heard" the voice of the people—only seemed to inflame the protesters. Your father, a successful businessman who owned land in central

Iran and a villa on the Caspian Sea, was accosted on the street one evening by an irate man who raised his fist at him, bared his teeth, and told him that he and the rest of the wealthy abusers in Iran would soon be kicked out of the country. When your father related the incident at the dinner table that night, you weren't sure if what you heard in his voice was humiliation, indignation, fear, or some combination of the three.

One afternoon shortly after the shouting began, you were sitting on the patio reading when you overheard a conversation between Mustapha, the houseboy, and his cousin Rahman. Mustapha had been brought in from a village when you were just a child and had lived for most of your life in a room in the basement of your house. Rahman had come to Tehran from the village to participate in the shouting. You could hear their voices coming from the back of the yard, where Mustapha was watering the geraniums, and you put your book down and listened. You didn't know at the time that the conversation would be permanently etched in your mind.

Rahman spoke first. "I don't know how you can continue to work as a houseboy, Mustapha-joon," he said. "How can we ever hope to advance as a country if villagers are going to keep being the slaves of the wealthy?"

"I am not a slave," Mustapha said.

"Yes, you are, my dear cousin. They brought you here from the village against your will—your father basically sold you to Agha. Just because you are paid a pittance doesn't mean that your job is dignified or fair. Nothing is fair under the Shah. And by the way, it's not just the Shah we must fight against. We must fight against wealthy landowners like your Agha too. All of them must go."

Here Rahman paused to allow his cousin to respond, but Mustapha remained silent. When Rahman spoke again, his voice was soft and reverent. "The prophet Mohammed was the world's first revolutionary, Mustapha-joon. Did you know that? He didn't just want to convert the world to Islam. He wanted equality and justice for all people."

The mention of Mohammed finally provoked a response from Mustapha. "Do you think the prophet would approve of throwing rocks and Molotov cocktails at innocent people? Isn't Islam supposed to be a religion of submission and peace?"

"Don't forget that Mohammad fought with weapons. He led an army of ten thousand Muslims to Mecca." This was an important point, and Rahman paused to allow his cousin to counter it. But Mustapha grew silent again, and Rahman continued. "I'm sure the prophet would agree with me that no one deserves as much wealth as Agha has. The Qur'an says it clearly: The flesh and body that is raised on unlawful sustenance shall not enter Paradise."

Confronted now with the Qur'an, Mustapha became defensive. "It is not unlawful sustenance, Rahman. Agha earns his money honestly. He works very hard. Sometimes he doesn't even come home until after midnight."

Rahman gave another disdainful chuckle. "Please, cousin. What Agha does can hardly be called work. For all you know, he could be an agent of the United States, the Great Satan. And he is an infidel too."

"Infidel or not, he is a good man. He and Khanoum have been very good to me. They pay me well, and I have many benefits."

"Oh, my poor cousin," Rahman said. "Do you think they truly care about you? They only treat you well because you wait on them hand and foot."

"I'm sorry, but that's just not true," Mustapha replied, his voice rising again in pitch. "Agha gives me many days off, and I have free time in the evenings too. Khanoum always tells me I work too hard. Sometimes she even takes over the work and tells me to go upstairs and rest. She has taught me how to do so many things, things that she learned in countries that are more advanced than ours! She is almost like a friend."

Hearing these words as you sat on the patio, you felt on the verge of tears. Mustapha had no idea you were listening, so the thoughts he expressed had to be genuine. He thought of your father as a good man, and of your mother as a friend. He would remain devoted to your family.

But you were wrong. Less than a week after this conversation took place, Mustapha left your parents' home and never returned.

One Friday about a month after Mustapha disappeared, thousands gathered in downtown Jaleh Square to protest the Pahlavi regime. Soldiers were sent to the square to disperse the crowd, and they arrived prepared for battle, with helmets on their heads and machine guns in their hands. The general who gave the order spoke live on television and insisted that the soldiers had fired warning shots into the air first, and only opened fire on the crowd after the warnings were ignored. According to the newscast, only sixty-four people had been killed, and just as many soldiers had been killed by snipers firing from buildings and treetops.

There was no footage of any protesters being killed, but your stomach churned as you sat in front of the television with your parents and watched the coverage. You couldn't help but wonder if Mustapha was there in the crowd, if he could have been one of the ones killed. You convinced yourself that this was not likely; that the odds were in his favor. And yet, sixty-four human beings had been gunned down. This was no longer just a momentary flare-up of anger against the Shah, but a dangerous groundswell you knew would keep growing. Your father's foul mood would grow along with it. Hunched over in front of the television with his teacup as he watched the Jaleh Square massacre, your father released a torrent of angry comments in uncharacteristically foul language. "Those bastards! Their mothers are still wiping their asses, but they think they know everything. I'd like to see one of those sons of whores run the country!" You didn't know whether he was referring to the protesters or the soldiers, but you didn't ask.

What you did do, a few weeks later, was sneak out of the house, claiming that you were studying for an exam with friends, and attend a protest yourself. You found it hard to raise your fist, and even harder to raise your voice to shout along with the protesters, to intone the dangerous words "Marg bar Shah! Death to the Shah!" But you liked the sound of this phrase echoing in your ears. It was a chorus you wanted to be a part of.

Young and idealistic, you were convinced this was a genuine uprising against oppression and American imperialism, that it was inevitable and just. A corrupt puppet regime like the Shah's could not sustain itself indefinitely; it was only a matter of time before a heroic man would emerge to lead the oppressed and downtrodden in an authentic rebellion against their tyrannical government. That man was Khomeini. Together with your school friends, you pored over revolutionary texts, studied Khomeini's background, and convinced yourselves that this powerful man, with his prophet-like appearance, his effortless wisdom, and his soft-spoken diatribes against the Great Satan, was the very revolutionary Iran needed.

Finally, after repeated calls to leave the country, the Shah boarded a plane for Egypt. In his farewell speech before he departed, he claimed, tearfully, to be leaving the country in God's hands. Two weeks after that, Khomeini flew from Paris to Tehran. It was a foggy morning in February, but the people of Tehran were in a joyous mood. No one bothered to go to work that day, since most of the city's residents were going to be in the streets to welcome their new spiritual leader.

The event was airing live, and once again you sat in front of the television with your parents to watch it. The cameraman kept the Air France plane in focus as it circled over the airport multiple times before landing to ensure that there were no tanks blocking the runway. His voice filled with ecstasy, the newscaster reported that there were at least five million people lining the streets to greet the Ayatollah, maybe even as many as seven million. These numbers were incomprehensible to you, but the bird's-eye view of the crowd on the television screen suggested they might be true. When the camera moved to the street view, you saw that in the crowd were young women and men, grandmothers and grandfathers, babies in arms and babies in strollers, workmen carrying shovels and pickaxes, children on the shoulders of their parents, people in tribal costumes who must have come from outside the city. They were packed so close together that you wondered how anyone could breathe. The chorus of "Allah-o-Akbar" was deafening even as it emanated from the television screen.

After the plane landed, the camera zoomed in on the man himself: Ayatollah Ruhollah Khomeini. You had seen many pictures of Khomeini, but you were not prepared for the aura that surrounded him as he emerged from the airplane door, dressed in his black robe and turban, and raised his hand to wave at the crowds. His expression was grim and there was not a trace of a smile on his lips; he was like a creature from another realm. When he took his first breath of Iranian air in fourteen years, it was as though the earth stopped spinning to honor the occasion.

Taking slow, deliberate steps and keeping his head down, Khomeini descended the stairs from the plane. The crowds were now in a frenzy, shouting "Allah-o-Akbar! Khomeini Rahbar! God is great! Khomeini is our commander!" and "Come, Mahdi, come!" suggesting that they believed Khomeini was the long-awaited Mahdi, the mythical descendent of Muhammed who would supposedly emerge from hiding to rescue the human race.

The February wind beat against the Ayatollah's heavy robes, billowing them outward. He grabbed the hand of the pilot who had accompanied him down the stairs to steady himself. Behind him, his son Ahmad lifted his arm protectively toward his father's back. Once he was on the tarmac, the camera swiveled toward the many journalists who had been standing there for hours, waiting to hear his first words. There was a flurry of questions from all sides, to which he gave simple, monosyllabic answers, most of them inaudible against the sounds of the shouting and the wind. Then a tall young journalist, a man who was clearly foreign, approached Khomeini. Suddenly, unaccountably, the shouting stopped. Even the wind seemed to stop as this man moved closer to the Ayatollah and extended his microphone toward his lips.

The journalist was accompanied by an Iranian interpreter, and it was toward this man, not the foreigner, that Khomeini first lifted his eyes. Realizing he wasn't going to have eye contact with the Ayatollah himself, the journalist looked toward the interpreter too. The question he asked was a simple one, perhaps one he had not intended to ask: "What are you feeling?"

Now Khomeini turned to look at the foreigner, his face as impassive as a block of marble, and stroked his long grey beard. "*Heech ehsassi nadaram,*" he mumbled. The interpreter dutifully translated: "I feel nothing."

Your first reaction when you heard these words was disbelief. But then your mind turned to Mustapha. You knew he was somewhere in that airless crowd, hanging on every word Khomeini uttered. To Mustapha, this response would be a perfect illustration of the Ayatollah's spiritual transcendence, his achievement of a plane of understanding other mortals could not begin to achieve.

Just as you were beginning to unravel this thought, your father stirred on the sofa beside you, and spoke. "All those years in Paris," he said, "and he is still a donkey." You didn't turn to look at your father, but there was a tremble in his voice, and you thought he might be crying. Suddenly, without turning, you felt his arm encircle your shoulders and pull you close. "*Bee-chareh shodeem, dokhtaram,*" he said. "We are doomed, my daughter."

A few months after installing himself as Supreme Leader, Khomeini decreed the hijab to be mandatory for all women everywhere but in their homes. In his opinion, which was soon to become law, women would be "naked" without it.

At first, the hijab was a novelty for you, almost like a game. You enjoyed the challenge of matching your headscarf to your outfit and draping it in a way that would highlight your beauty. But the first time you saw your mother standing in front of the hall mirror and tying her headscarf under her chin, the full impact of the Islamic Revolution hit you all at once. You watched in awe as she fastened the headscarf under her jawline, pulling it so tightly that she looked like a medieval nun wearing a wimple. She saw you watching her and turned to reassure you. "Why are you staring at me like that?" she said. "I don't mind wearing a headscarf. Actually, I kind of like it. It eliminates the problem of what to wear and how to fix my hair."

Her voice was lighthearted, and you knew her well enough to know she was sincere. No matter what came her way, she would adjust. But when she turned back toward you, it seemed to you that her head had shrunk and that she herself had grown smaller.

That July, five months after Khomeini's return, you boarded an Iran Air jet alone and streaked across the sky to the literal other side of the planet. In the country you left behind, voters had overwhelmingly approved the creation of an Islamic Republic, a Revolutionary Guard Corps and a morality police had been established, and a constitution had been approved giving Khomeini absolute and unlimited power. In the country you were traveling to, a nuclear reactor had recently melted down and spewed radioactive gases into the air, a dollar coin had been issued depicting the face of a women's rights activist, and McDonald's had just released its first Happy Meal. You didn't know any of this, or knew it only fuzzily, anecdotally, like something you could see through the windows of a car that was moving too fast for you to retain any of its details.

The decision to leave home was neither willful nor forced; it was merely inevitable. You would be joining the hordes of young, moneyed Iranians who had the privilege of leaving the country when it wasn't to their liking. Though your parents cried when you left, they recognized that life in Iran was suffocating for a budding woman; if you remained, your only hope for stability was an arranged marriage to a doctor or an engineer who could protect you from the wantonness you were inclined to and from the scrutiny of the morality police.

The man you wanted to marry was a man your parents didn't know existed, a man you had been meeting with on the sly, who had introduced to you Plato and Aristotle, and later to Marx and Lenin. After he was arrested and thrown into Evin Prison, his mother called you secretly to tell you he planned to marry you when he was released and wanted you to wait for him. You agreed to meet her at a grocery store down the street from your house. She arrived holding a box with an engagement ring inside. You hugged her, took the ring out of the box, and put it on right away. You wore it for a while after arriving in the United States, but when the hope of your beloved's release faded, you took it off and kept it in the nightstand of your dorm room until you looked for it one day and noticed it had vanished.

When you arrived in the new world, it was you who felt new. You didn't recognize yourself in the desirable, exotic woman you became in the eyes of others. The women you met mistrusted your exoticism; the men wanted to claim it and wave it around for other men to see. You ignored the women at first and later won them over with kindness. You succumbed to the men at first and later cultivated a haughty, icy vibe that kept them at bay until they began to succumb to you. Gradually, you adopted a when-in-Rome attitude. You never bothered to count your lovers, never thought twice before experimenting with the many drugs that were offered to you, never once paused to consider the obvious inconsistencies between your professed ideology and your behavior.

As far as your studies, you dabbled: some Russian literature, some Nietzsche and Kierkegaard, some comparative East-West philosophy, some African art. You meditated. You volunteered as a test subject in a sleep lab. You moved in and out of the campus political scene, but activists soon started to feel phony to you, especially when they cried crocodile tears about the events in Iran, a country whose name they mispronounced.

At the beginning of your sophomore year, Iraqi bombs began to fall on Iran. You knew the bombs weren't likely to fall on your parents' home, which was safely nestled beneath the mountains to the north of the city, but you were shaken by the stories they told you of seeking shelter in the basement when they heard the anti-aircraft sirens. Lying in your dorm room at night, you often found yourself recreating the sounds of the bombs in your head. On the nights when the moon shone full outside your window, you sometimes had the sensation that the moonlight was an afterglow from an explosion. Then you would bury your head in the pillow you had brought from home—a pillow that still smelled faintly of your bedroom in Tehran—until the moon descended and the sounds subsided.

Gradually, you learned to tune out the sounds of the bombs by replacing them with other sounds. The punk movement was at its peak, and its aesthetic appealed to you. You didn't pierce your body or dye your hair, but you were drawn to the angry, anti-establishment lyrics, and you blasted punk rock music loudly in your dorm room. Although you had nothing in common with punk rockers in most ways, you flitted about on the fringes of their cliques without ever fully entering them. If nothing else, it was an interesting vantage point from which to observe human nature. You would turn the lights off in your dorm room, lie down in your bed, and belt out the music of The Dead Kennedys:

Gonna kill, kill, kill, kill, kill the poor
Kill, kill, kill, kill, kill the poor

ॐ

The shouting began again three decades later, when you were forty-seven. It wasn't the first time there had been shouting since you had left the country, but it was the loudest and most promising in thirty years. This time, there was hope. The hope was alive not only on the streets of Tehran, but as far away as the United States, where it made the front pages of newspapers and magazines.

By the time the shouting came again, you were fully ensconced in your life in America. It still sometimes shocked you to realize that you had now lived longer in your adopted country than in the country of your birth. In the prosaic words of one of your Iranian friends, you had "fallen into life in America like a pig falls into mud." Your local pharmacist knew you. The woman at the tag office knew you. Your doctor had seen you through birth control, birth, and perimenopause. Your hairdresser had seen you through the process of your hair beginning to grey. The same mechanic had worked on your cars for decades.

You had been married to an American man named Daniel Logan for nearly twenty years, and together you had two children who were, at the time the shouting began, in their teens. The four of you lived in a house in Woodstock, Georgia, twenty-five miles north of Atlanta. Atlanta had a sizable Iranian community, and you flitted in and out of it like you had done with the punk rock movement. Your children had a few Iranian friends and spoke a bit of pidgin Farsi. You raised them on homecooked Persian dishes, introduced them to Persian music, and told them stories about your youth in Iran before the Revolution. They seemed to be as well-adjusted as any other adolescents, even though they were carrying around DNA from two ethnicities that were perpetually at odds.

Until you met Danny, you had mostly given up on men. They all wanted the wrong things from you. The Iranian ones wanted you to be a duplicate of their sainted mothers, even though some of them espoused ideas of gender equality. The ethnic ones were focused on image and wanted you as an unconventional, alluring showpiece to accompany their own exoticism. The American ones were the worst. They pretended to be interested in your heritage, but they secretly wanted you to repress all the Iranian parts of yourself and to become just another American woman, albeit with dark hair and a weird last name. Some of them couldn't find Iran on a map and had only vague, media-fed ideas about it. One American man you dated, upon hearing the shouts of "Allah-o-Akbar" that rang out from the rooftops in Iran, asked you, "Why are they saying *Hello, Akbar?* Who is Akbar, anyway?"

Your experiences with men always put you in mind of Picasso's famous sentence about women being one of two things: either goddesses or doormats. Though you didn't know what you wanted to be to a man, you knew it was neither of those.

When you met Danny at the birthday party of a colleague, you were instantly enthralled by him. He was gorgeous in the way only an

American man can be—lean and muscular, with an unruly mane of blond hair and sparkling eyes that had a permanent look of wonder in them. Your heart palpitated as you stood face to face under the porch light of your friend's house and conversed, red wine in hand. You allowed yourself to drift away in his ocean-blue eyes and scanned his suntanned, athletic body up and down as he bent to pick up the shrimp that, in your nervousness, had fallen from the toothpick in your hand.

It wasn't just Danny's physical presence that had pulled you in. You were transfixed by his effortless candor, his dismissive comments about the "losers" he had grown up with in Georgia; his humble working-class background; his determination to work his way through college and become a high school history teacher; his incisive judgments about the state of the world. You had never known anyone like him. Danny instantly wormed his way into a part of you that you didn't know existed, awakening both your feminine desires and your yearnings for rebellion against the repressive, scripted existence you had hitherto been living. You had read your Marx and Engels, your Rousseau, and your Nietzsche. Danny was all of their visions rolled into one and wrapped in sexy packaging: a working-class hero, a diamond in the rough, a noble savage, and an übermensch.

Danny had a restless mind that was hungry for something different, something daring, something that would stretch his boundaries and test his mettle. The fact that Iranians were hostile to Americans made him even more determined to conquer you and become a permanent fixture in your life. His interest was genuine when he asked you about the Islamic Republic, about what your life had been like in Iran before the Revolution, about your hopes for your country's future. He tried his best to verse himself in the Iranian political situation, not only to impress you, but also because it gave him a feeling of superiority to think that he was able to see truth, while his fellow

Americans were hopelessly misled by hateful, one-sided propaganda. He even defended the taking of hostages, insisting that it was a legitimate act of defiance against American imperialism. He was half in love with the beautiful young woman who had courageously broken the lock on the embassy gate with a pair of metal cutters she had hidden under her chador. The hostages, Danny argued, were merely "payback." After all, they weren't being mistreated—and when they were released and returned safely to their suburban homes in the States, they would get all book contracts and well-paid speaking tours. "It's the best thing that ever happened to them," he gushed. "It's the best thing that ever happened to that loser Ted Koppel, too."

This was going a bit too far, and you felt the need to correct him. "It's barbaric," you said. "How can you glamorize a bunch of illiterate children who don't even have facial hair yet, but think they can control world politics simply because someone put a Kalashnikov in their hands?"

Danny merely smiled. "Calm down, baby," he said. "All's fair in love and war."

He practiced saying the words Marg bar Amreeka, knowing full well that they meant "Death to America." For some reason, he found this amusing, and he began to apply the phrase marg bar to just about everything. He had never liked baseball, preferring football instead. "*Marg bar* baseball," he would say. On a hot day, he would mumble, "*Marg bar* this damned heat." When he didn't feel like going to work, he would say, "*Marg bar* work!" His best application of the expression came during a picnic the two of you were having in Piedmont Park. When flies started swarming around your food, he shouted, "*Marg bar* flies! Death to flies!" and began swatting at them with a napkin.

Even after nearly twenty years of marriage, Danny still softened your heart. He was a good man, a good husband, and a good father.

And when the shouting began the second time, Danny was right where you needed him to be. He never pushed you to talk about it, but he listened if you felt like talking.

This time, you were too far away to imagine that the shouting was happening right outside your window. Instead, you felt it pulsing through your system, pounding inside you like the reverb in an amplifier that was too close. This time, the shouting wasn't directed *at* you or at your parents. Instead, it seemed to be happening *for* you.

It started because the protesters believed the election that returned Ahmadinejad to power had been rigged. Ahmadinejad had the forehead of a monkey and the eyes of a snake, and whenever you saw a picture of him or heard him speak, you felt a wave of revulsion mixed with a stab of dread. There was no doubt in your mind that the election had indeed been rigged. How could it not be? Ahmadinejad was announced the winner only hours after the polls closed, before there was time to count even a fraction of the votes.

Your Iranian friends in Atlanta were ecstatic when the shouting began again. They felt a sense of solidarity with the shouters, even though their parents had fled the country when they were children and most of them had only visited as wealthy tourists. One of your closest Iranian friends, a diasporan like you, was so excited that she decided to return to Iran for the first time in years. Lululemon had recently introduced a full line of Islamic clothing for women, and she ordered an expensive silk hijab and bought a tacky pink handbag to go with it. She went to Walmart before leaving and bought colored pencils for the children in the family, cheap makeup for the women, and cheap cologne for the men, thinking these items could not be purchased in Iran. Her family members were deeply insulted by the gifts. This woman, like many of your Iranian friends, was hopelessly ignorant about Iran, but ignorantly hopeful about the protests. She was so fired up that one would think she herself was on the streets protesting, when in fact she was polishing her nails in her comfortable home in Buckhead.

Your American friends reacted to the shouting with remarks ranging from feigned interest to ill-informed opinions to expressions of solidarity that had a Southern "bless-your-heart" tone to them. They said things like, "It must be really hard for you to be here when all of that is going on!" or asked weak questions like, "So, what exactly IS going on over there? Do you think it will get anywhere?" Some of them wanted to tell *you* what was going on, and offered ridiculous opinions like, "Israel and the CIA are probably behind it all."

Danny got it when no one else could. With him you were able to express your complex tangle of feelings: your cautious hope, your sense of detachment, your worry, your desire to be present to witness what might finally be the death of the Islamic Republic. Danny encouraged you to travel to Iran. It was May, and school was about to close. The kids were old enough to get by without you. You hadn't been back to Iran in almost a decade, since your father passed away and you traveled to Iran to help your mother move to the States.

A few months into the shouting, a phone call came from a male cousin in Iran. His voice was filled with optimism as he tried to convince you to come back to join the protests. "This movement is historic," he said. "You are going to be sorry if you miss it. And when you come, make sure you bring a good cell phone with you. Everyone is taking pictures and videos and posting them on Twitter. The bastards are trying to shut down the Twitter feeds coming out of Iran, but a young American man named Austin has figured out how to set up a proxy server so we can bounce our connection through another country. It's brilliant! We can hide encrypted data inside our own government's communications. If the sons of whores only knew how we are tricking them." You felt a lump in your throat as you listened to your cousin's impassioned words, and you couldn't sleep for days afterward. A few weeks later, you packed your bags and flew to Tehran.

You hired a taxi to take you from Imam Khomeini International Airport to your cousin's apartment in downtown Tehran. As you traveled through the city, all your senses were bombarded at once, and you were ambushed with a series of Proustian memories. The cab careened, making nausea-producing arcs through the winding streets. The windows were all open, allowing the heavy city air to waft through the cab, bringing with it an amalgam of odors that was discomfiting, but somehow smelled like home: the muddy water flowing through the *jubes* that lined the side of each street; the steam from the corner laundries that was let out into the street at regular intervals; the overripe, unsold fruit that had been abandoned by ambulant vendors the previous day; the exhaust from the sea of angry cars.

The cacophony of sounds was equally overwhelming, and these, too, awakened memories that had been sleeping inside you for years. The driver's angry outbursts through his open window could barely be heard above the din of car horns, screeching brakes, and the frenetic movements of every conceivable mode of transportation, from baby strollers to double-decker buses, from shiny Mercedes Benzes to donkey carts. There were happy, busy sounds of people going about their daily business, shuffling down the street carrying bags full of groceries, yelling at their children to watch out for the traffic, haggling with the salesmen at the fruit stands. Tehran was every bit as alive as you remembered it.

The sights you saw through the cab window were shocking but uplifting. Tehran was far more colorful than any American could possibly imagine, having only seen media images of the city which depicted it as monochromatic and grey. Spread across the brick walls along the streets were portraits of Imam Khomeini and various other figures, garishly painted in sizes much larger than life. No matter how one felt about the subject matter of the murals or the slogans beneath them, they were impressive in terms of technique, and their colors accosted the eye. Along the street in front of the murals were brightly colored signs and marquees announcing a surprising variety of products and services: travel agencies in neon blue, ice cream parlors and bakeries in screaming yellow and orange, clothing stores in trendy turquoise and magenta.

Two days after arriving, you went out into the streets with your cousin to join a protest. Once again, the crowd was eclectic: young men holding children on their shoulders, adolescents dressed in jeans and sweatshirts, businessmen dressed in suits. The uprising was now being called "the green movement," after the theme color of the opposition party, and everywhere you looked, you saw green. Many of the protesters were wearing green shirts and scarves, and some had streaked their faces with green paint. Although the women in the crowd were wearing the mandatory hijab, most of them had draped their scarves loosely about their shoulders, exposing lots of hair. Every person you had eye contact with smiled and held up two fingers in a victory sign.

About an hour into the protest, you noticed thick black smoke rising from somewhere not too far away, and you pushed forward to see what was causing it. You identified the source by smell rather than by sight: it was the distinct odor of burning tires. You couldn't get a clear view of the intersection, but you could see several people standing on the tops of parked cars. Some of them were shouting through megaphones, but the noise around you was so intense that you could not make out what they were saying. Arms were reaching toward these speakers from all directions—arms ending in fists, arms ending in victory signs, arms draped in green sashes, arms that had been dipped in red paint to look like they were covered in blood. You glanced up at the balconies of the apartments surrounding the square and saw that they, too, were brimming with people. Everywhere you looked, there was a veritable sea of cell phones.

Suddenly the crowd began to sway and shout in unison: "MARG BAR DIKTATOR! Death to the dictator!" The words caught in your throat at first, but after a few tries, your voice welled up from a place deep inside you and the words came rushing out. It gave you chills to be saying these words so freely.

You tilted your head back to look up at the sky, bright blue and cloudless. You closed your eyes to shield them from the sun, and your head began to spin. And then, with your eyes still closed, you felt yourself being pushed forward. There was nothing you could do but surrender to the movement. It was like being in a river and being pulled along by the current, resisting enough to stay alive, but trusting the river to carry you to where you needed to go. The sensation was unnerving but exhilarating.

Your impulse was to pull out your cell phone and film, even though you didn't know where you were going and had no idea what you might be filming. You lifted your cell phone into the air, pressed the video button, and recorded. Without looking at your recordings, you searched for Austin's proxy connection and sent them out.

Back at your cousin's home that evening, you scrolled through the videos you had taken. In one of them, you thought you could see a woman in the distance hoisting herself up onto a barrel, ripping off her headscarf, and raising her fist in the air. Another video captured a man dangling from a balcony and then dropping down into the crowd below, where he was caught by a network of human hands. A third clip captured a huge green banner being lifted into the air and flapping in the wind over the protesters' heads.

But there was one video clip you kept coming back to, pausing, rewinding, and enlarging it to puzzle it out. What you had captured was a sudden rush of people toward a side street, accompanied by the loud tattoo of gunfire, followed by wailing. Someone had been shot no more than twenty meters from where you were standing.

You were too far away to record the incident itself, but in the days that followed, it became evident what you had caught on film: a woman named Neda Agha-Soltan, a beautiful young college student and aspiring musician, had been shot and killed at the protest while walking back to her car. Eyewitnesses insisted that she had been shot by an armed guard who took aim at her from a rooftop. Government officials first said that she had not been shot at all; that she was still alive. But there were many other onlooker videos of the incident, some of them much clearer than yours. After the footage went viral on social media and was aired on CNN, the government changed its story, first saying the footage was fake, then blaming the killing on someone else—a BBC reporter, the CIA, the leftist groups who had attended the protest.

By the time you left Iran a few weeks later, the shouting had all but disappeared. In the plane on the way back to Atlanta, you were reminded of a Farsi expression you had heard all your life: "Same yogurt, different bowl."

&

This time, the shouting began with the death of a woman. She was a feisty and brilliant twenty-two-year-old who had just been admitted to university to study law. She died on your sixtieth birthday. You didn't know about her death on that day, but when you learned about it later, you calculated that you were in Savannah enjoying a birthday dinner with Danny at the very moment she perished.

Although there were again multiple versions of the event, the basic facts could not be disputed. A young Kurdish woman named Mahsa Amini was arrested by the Guidance Patrol for a hijab violation while visiting her brother in Tehran. Her brother was with her when she was arrested and watched her being thrown into the back of a van. The men who took her reassured him that his sister would be taken temporarily to a detention center to receive instruction about proper Islamic dress, and then she would be released. No one witnessed what happened to her inside the van, but by the time she arrived at the police station, she had lost consciousness. Two hours after the arrest, she was transported by ambulance to the intensive care unit of a Tehran hospital. She was in a coma for two days, during which time the news of her condition got out on Twitter. By the time she died, her story had sent shockwaves throughout the world. The shouting began just hours after her death.

This time, the shouting is strident, rabid, and relentless. It comes at you from your television, your cell phone, your car radio, your computer, your smart watch, your smart speaker. You hear it everywhere you go, as if in surround sound. It is echoing around the world, and you are engulfed in it. You cannot tune it out or unhear it.

It feels different this time. People you barely know reach out to you, send you articles, call you to talk about the protests, inform themselves, want to get involved. The principal of the school where you teach asks you to speak about the uprising in morning assembly. Your colleagues, suddenly remembering that you are an Iranian woman, begin to look at you with admiration. Friends from Europe send you clips of celebrities and authorities in their countries making bold statements in solidarity with the protesters. Stephen Colbert and Trevor Noah do segments on the shouting, and even Bill Maher interviews an Iranian female journalist. Facebook and social media sites are inundated with images of the protests and reports about the atrocities being committed in response. UN delegates from all over the world declare their sympathy with the protesters at the General Assembly and urge world leaders to take action. Yes, it is different this time.

At first, you are mesmerized by this new wave of shouting, and it makes you feel buoyant and hopeful. But soon, another feeling overtakes you: you sink into a kind of numbness, a state of funk. You can't watch the news from Iran, and you can't *not* watch it. You don't know what kind of action to take, but you can't *not* take action.

You cut your hair in solidarity with the protesters. You break your vow never to post on social media and post daily news reports about the protests on your Facebook page. Young men and women buy WOMAN, LIFE, FREEDOM T-shirts and wear them proudly to their schools and workplaces. You plan elaborate lessons for your students with video footage of the protests followed by provocative questions. You pay for a subscription to the *Washington Post* because it provides a daily update on the movement. Your daughter, now in her early thirties, plans a poetry reading featuring the works of Iranian female poets. Your son, who is twenty-six and an accomplished musician, plays the anthem "Baraye" over and over and writes his own song about the protests. There is a rally at Centennial Olympic Park, and you and Danny take part in it.

But you do not go to Iran. There are many good reasons not to go: Covid is still rampant. Flights are expensive. You have very few family members left in the country, so you have nowhere to stay. The streets of Iran are not safe. You could be accused of spying and end up in prison. You are old, and you are afraid.

But the real reason you don't travel to Iran is fear of a different kind. It is fear of yourself. Fear that you are an impostor. Fear that you do not fully grasp the many grievances of the shouters, and that they will know this the minute they see you. Fear that your Farsi has atrophied and that you can no longer express yourself comfortably in your native language. Fear that you no longer understand what it means to be Iranian. Fear that you no longer understand yourself.

Alongside your fear, you feel shame. You are ashamed of having grown up as a member of an elite class who waved away the injustice even as they contributed to it. You are ashamed of once believing that Khomeini was the answer. You are ashamed of having lived longer outside of your country than in it. You are ashamed of the comfortable, storybook American life you have built, when such a life is beyond reach for so many in your country. You are ashamed of having dedicated your life to teaching American children instead of Iranian children. You are ashamed of not transferring your Iranian heritage to your own children, thus setting in motion its inevitable demise.

This shouting has made you aware, suddenly and painfully, that the roots you have put down in your adopted country have not fully taken hold. Long-lost parts of you are suddenly creeping back, clamoring for your attention after decades of neglect—and when you pay attention to them, you realize you have become nothing more than a pale imitation of the Iranian woman you once were. You want to believe that Iran is still alive in you, that it is not watered down to the point where it is just an anecdote, a story you tell, a badge you take out and wear when the occasion calls for it.

In the wake of this new, urgent shouting, you have come to the shocking realization that your Iranian heritage now exists mostly in the realm of memory. It feels hollow to recount your memories, exhausting even to hold them. Try as you might, you cannot seem to balance your fading memories in one hand and this powerful shouting in the other. You will inevitably stumble in the attempt, and each time you do, your shame will resurface.

Perhaps the heaviest emotion that this new shouting has sparked in you is something akin to survivor's guilt. You feel guilty for being alive when so many have died; guilty for hoping the shouting will continue even though it means that more people will be imprisoned, tortured, and executed; guilty for expecting others to risk their lives

to pave the way for you to return to a place you love but have abandoned; guilty because it is far too easy for you to applaud the women
who are bravely stripping off their hijab and going out into the streets
to face tanks and machine guns, when you have never had to do that,
and never will.

Your fear, your shame, and your guilt will help nothing and no
one. The best you can do is to feed them into words on paper, so at
least they will feel real.

ABOUT THE AUTHOR

S UZI EHTESHAM-ZADEH IS THE daughter of an Iranian father and an American mother and grew up in Tehran under the Shah. She moved to California to attend Stanford University, but when the Islamic Revolution started brewing shortly after she graduated, she returned to Iran and plopped herself down in it, remaining there for the first few years of the Khomeini regime. She later spent several years in Europe before settling in the United States. A lifelong English teacher, Suzi has taught in schools and universities on three continents and in three languages. Her fiction has appeared in numerous publications, including *The Georgia Review*, *Narrative Northeast*, *Gertrude Press*, and *Fiction International*. She holds a BA in Philosophy from Stanford University and an MFA in Creative Writing from Boston University. She currently resides on a six-acre farm in Woodstock, Georgia.

ACKNOWLEDGMENTS

Wʜᴇɴ I ʙᴇɢᴀɴ ᴛᴏ compose a list of the people who
helped to bring this book about, I was reminded of
the discussions in my college philosophy classes on the
metaphysics of causality: the conundrum about whether any one
event can ever be isolated as the cause of any other. I find I am unable
to isolate the "causes" of this book because each of them can be traced
back to another, earlier cause. Some of the stories in *Zan* were written
recently and quickly, while others, it seems, have been in the works
throughout my life. For the purposes of brevity, I have settled on a
list of the most immediate and undeniable forces that have shaped
this book—the people without whom I am certain it never would
have happened. I will make no attempt to order them temporally or
to rank them in importance.

My wonderful, brilliant sisters, Miriam and Ariane Ehtesham,
were early readers of these stories and have followed them through
their many changes. Their sharp insights, their boundless sororal
love, and their ongoing validation of my writing have been essential
fuels that have kept my engine running.

Two fellow writers, Maija Makinen and Georgina Parfitt, have
remained invested in *Zan* since it first started to take shape in our
creative writing classes at Boston University. Maija and Georgina,

both highly accomplished writers whose work I am humbled by, have deconstructed these stories with me countless times. Their honest and incisive comments have greatly improved them, and I am eternally thankful for their guidance and their friendship.

It goes without saying that I am thankful to everyone at Dzanc Books who read *Zan* and believed in it. Chelsea Gibbons was the first to edit the manuscript, and she did so with just the right balance of enthusiasm and clear-eyed critique. I am grateful to Steven Seighman for the many gorgeous cover designs he created and for patiently putting up with my demands until we settled on the perfect one.

Dzanc's amazing editor-in-chief, Michelle Dotter, deserves a paragraph of her own. I am convinced Michelle is the best editor in the country. Her passion for writing is deep and genuine, her judgment is unerring, her knowledge is vast, and she is gently and quietly forceful. I cannot calculate how many hours (weeks? months?) Michelle spent poring over my book, but I honestly believe she now knows my stories better than I do.

I owe a huge debt to my Iranian family members—those who remain in Iran and those who are scattered across the planet. Although they have not played a direct part in bringing *Zan* about, I have borrowed from their experiences and from my memories of the rich and stimulating years we spent together in our beloved homeland.

Finally, I acknowledge the twin poles of my life: my parents and my children. My daughter, Asia Meana, is my soulmate, my closest confidante in all things emotional and literary, and my paragon of both scholarship and creativity. My son, Elias Meana, is my energy source, my intellectual sparring partner, and my shining example of a powerful mind coupled with a compassionate heart. My father, Dr. Teymour Ehtesham-Zadeh, no longer dwells on the Earth in living form, but he is alive, in some form, on every page of this book. My mother, Sarah Kale Ehtesham-Zadeh, is my model of ideal womanhood, my best friend, my favorite person, and the "first cause" of all of the above.

To the many, many others I have left out: I hope you know who you are and can feel my gratitude.